FATAL LEGACY

Literary gatherings are not Sheila Malory's cup of tea but when her old friend Dame Elizabeth Blackmore invites her to a Writer of the Year party Sheila accepts. A week later Sheila learns that Beth has died suddenly, and that she has been appointed Beth's literary executor.

Among Beth's papers is an unfinished novel about a passionate love affair, which Sheila is convinced is autobiographical. Could her friend have been living a double life? And why are her children Helen and Mark behaving so strangely?

Then an academic researching the novelist's life also dies suddenly, and Sheila begins to suspect that Beth's death was no accident...

FATAL LEGACY

FATAL LEGACY

by

Hazel Holt

Magna Large Print Books
Long Preston, North Yorkshire,
BD23 4ND, England.

British Library Cataloguing in Publication Data.

Holt, Hazel
    Fatal legacy.

    A catalogue record of this book is
    available from the British Library

    ISBN   0-7505-1620-8

First published in Great Britain by Macmillan
an imprint of Macmillan Publishers Ltd., 1999

Copyright © Hazel Holt, 1999

The right of Hazel Holt to be identified as the author of this
work has been asserted by her in accordance with the
Copyright, Designs and Patents Act, 1988

Published in Large Print 2000 by arrangement with
Macmillan Publishers Limited

Magna Large Print is an imprint of Library Magna Books Ltd.

Printed and bound in Great Britain by
T.J. (International) Ltd., Cornwall, PL28 8RW

For Ruth and Gerry
who also live with cats

Let's choose executors, and talk of wills...

Richard II

Chapter One

'I really think you ought to go, Ma,' Michael said. 'You'll enjoy it when you get there – as you used to say about those ghastly children's parties you made me go to.'

'Oh, I don't know–'

He picked up the card and studied it. '"Writer of the Year"! Lots of people would give their eye teeth!'

'It means going to London,' I protested.

'You know you *love* going up to London.'

I don't very often go to literary parties. I never seem to know anyone there and, although I've written several books (about nineteenth-century novelists), I still find it hard to think of myself as a Real Author, so I always feel self-conscious and out of place.

'Many are called,' Michael said reprovingly, 'but few are chosen.'

'Oh well,' I said. 'I'll see.'

I probably wouldn't have gone even then if it hadn't been for a letter from my friend Beth saying that *she* was going and wouldn't it be nice to meet there and go for a meal together afterwards. Beth is an old friend, we were up at Oxford together. She is, in fact, Dame Elizabeth Blackmore and a very eminent novelist indeed. I don't see her very often nowadays, but we've always kept in touch.

The party was held in one of the larger London bookshops and when I arrived I *didn't* know anybody there, so I took the proffered glass of wine and wandered round, examining the titles on the shelves to cover up the fact that I had no one to talk to. Glancing sideways at the crowd, all talking with what seemed to me like excessive animation, I recognized several well-known faces, not only from the world of literature, but also from broadcasting, politics and what might loosely be called show business, and I reflected that *writing* a book was the easy bit.

I listened to the conversation around me.

'...he said it was a six-figure advance, but what he *didn't* say was that it was a two-book contract!...'

'...I know the royalties were up on last time, but the advance was just the same, so it was really a cop-out–'

'...and she was actually registered for VAT and now that the threshold's been raised she must be making a packet!...'

I wonder if at a gathering of accountants they talk about literature. Probably not.

I made a little sortie into the room and found myself face to face with Ursula Carton, the well-known biographer, who had given my recent book on Mrs Oliphant a perfectly horrible review. We exchanged glances of mutual dislike and she plunged abruptly back into the crowd, while I resumed my examination of the bookshelves. I was just considering the immense amount of shelf space devoted to books on oriental cookery, when a voice behind me said, 'I might have known that you'd be early! You always did arrive at things *hours* before anyone else!'

'And I've spent some of the best years of my life waiting for you!'

Beth has never looked her age and in the elegantly draped little black dress that set off her still bright chestnut hair she looked really stunning.

'Goodness,' I said, 'don't you look splendid! Is that a Jean Muir?'

'Expensive but timeless, dear,' she replied, retrieving from the past the phrase we always used when we bought garments we couldn't really afford.

Nowadays, though, Beth can afford most things. Not only is she a highly successful novelist (with several books made into films), but she is also married to a very wealthy businessman. We were all surprised when Beth married John Blackmore – her previous boyfriends had been more eccentric, flamboyant even – and even her fiercest critics (and there are always plenty of *them* in the literary world) never suggested that she was marrying for money. Over the years, though, I've come to appreciate the qualities Beth recognized in John. His humour, kindness and calm good sense have carried her through the bad time (they lost their first son when he was just six months old) as well as helping her to cope with the quite different stresses of her success.

'It's *lovely* to see you again,' Beth exclaimed. 'It's been far too long. You really should come up to London more often instead of vegetating in the country.'

'I rather like vegetating,' I protested. 'Anyway, you know how it is – things pile up and there never seems to be time for anything except the bare essentials. As it is, I can hardly squeeze in the odd bit of writing.'

'Too many good works,' Beth said. 'People take advantage.'

'When you live in a small town, you *have* to be involved. It's been worse, really, since Peter died. I suppose I threw myself into things to keep occupied and now I'm sort of stuck with them. And then, of course, there's Michael.'

'How is he?'

'Oh, fine. He's an assistant solicitor now. You know he went into Peter's old firm? I think he really enjoys the law. I'm awfully lucky that he wants to live in Taviscombe and that he still likes living at home. He's splendid company.'

'But hard work, I bet! Children always are, however old they get!'

'You sound a bit sour,' I said. 'Problems with your two?'

'Don't ask!' Beth groaned.

I wasn't able to pursue the subject because several people came up wanting to talk to Beth. She introduced me to them, but I soon found myself edging out of the conversation because my feet were aching and my back was beginning to give out from standing so long. I was just looking round for a chair, or at least a suitable ledge to lean on, when a voice behind me said, 'Fancy seeing you here!'

The voice, familiar from ministerial pronouncements on the radio and television, but also familiar in more frivolous circumstances in our youth, made me exclaim with pleasure.

'Bill! Bill North! How lovely to see you after all this time!'

He had certainly changed since our Oxford days. Gone were the baggy corduroys and leather-patched jacket, the polo sweater and the shoulder-length blond hair, and in their place a suit from Savile Row, a shirt from Jermyn Street and a Garrick Club tie. His hair, neatly cut (probably at Trumpers), was definitely receding. But the smile, the old, warm, Bill North smile remained the same.

'Congratulations on your Cabinet appointment,' I said. 'I was going to write to you, but it's been so long, and you've become so grand, I thought you might not remember me!'

'Come off it, Sheila!'

'Well, you *have* done well. The next Prime Minister – isn't that what the political journalists keep saying?'

Bill laughed. 'My age is against me,' he said. 'Over forty, perhaps; over fifty, no way!'

He hailed a girl carrying drinks. 'Over here, love!' He took two new glasses of wine and handed one to me. 'God knows what this is, but it's certainly an improvement on that Algerian red we used to drink.'

'You always drank beer,' I said. 'I don't think wine went with your image!'

'It was fun, though, wasn't it? Do you remember that last night party after Guy's production of *Troilus and Cressida*? When Terry got absolutely smashed and climbed into old Jerrold's room – he was the Dean of Corpus – and passed out on his sofa? And Gordon climbed in after him and filled the place with balloons!'

'That was the evening,' I said, 'when Anita Warburg decided she was madly in love with you and followed you all the way along the

High, sobbing her heart out because you'd gone off with Lois Spencer.'

'God, yes! I'd forgotten that! I wonder what happened to her? Lois, I mean. Anita went to America I believe and married a millionaire, so I don't suppose she ever thinks of me now!'

'Oh, she probably has fond memories,' I said. 'The loves of one's youth always seem sweet in retrospect! Anyway, it's marvellous to see you so well and flourishing.'

'I'm not the only one,' Bill said, looking at Beth. '*She's* done pretty well, wouldn't you say? A Dame, if you please! '

'Oh, Beth always was terrifically bright.'

'No brighter than you,' Bill said. 'We always thought you were going to be an academic highflyer. But then you went off into the wilds of Devon.'

'Somerset,' I corrected him. 'No, my mother was ill for a long time and then I was married and my son was born... Actually, looking around at my academic friends, I'm very glad to be out of *that* particular rat race! I'm quite happy doing the odd article and writing the occasional book.'

'I read your last one – I thought it was excellent.'

I looked at him in surprise and he laughed.

'You don't have to be illiterate to be a politician – though I have to admit that at times it helps!'

'Don't be an idiot,' I said. 'It's just that I didn't think nineteenth-century novelists were your particular cup of tea. And I certainly admired *your* book. One always forgets that you were an historian before you were a politician–'

I stopped speaking as a tall woman, in her thirties I should imagine, came up behind Bill and slipped her hand through his arm. As I looked more closely, I recognized her (from newspaper photographs since I'd never met her) as his wife. She had blonde hair cut short and flipped up at the side and she was wearing a beautifully cut suit, though in a rather trying shade of lime green (*Vogue's* must-have colour for the season) and expensive-looking shoes with very high heels, which I felt were a mistake for someone of her height. She somehow gave the impression of a woman who'd been 'made over' by some magazine to look fashionable and who was ill at ease and uncomfortable about the whole affair.

Bill acknowledged her presence and said to me, 'This is Anne – I don't think you two have met. Anne, this is Sheila Malory, an old and dear Oxford friend.'

She shook my extended hand and gave me a brief smile. 'Lovely to meet you,' she said. 'Bill, dear,' she went on, 'it's gone eight o'clock and I did tell Nanny we'd be back by half-past – you know I promised Charlotte that she could stay up until we got home and I don't want it to be too late.'

'You have a Nanny!' I exclaimed. The concept of Bill with such a domestic appendage seemed so unlikely.

'*And* three children,' he said.

'Oh, I wasn't criticizing,' I protested. 'In

fact, I think everyone should have a loving and efficient Nanny provided by the State. You should put that in your next manifesto – you'd sweep the country!'

'Good idea! It wouldn't be any more far-fetched than some of the things in our last one.'

He saw Anne frowning and said, 'Joke, love, joke.'

'What ages are your children?' I asked Anne, trying to make some sort of contact.

'Charlotte's the eldest, she's eight, then Blanche is six and Robert's two.'

'How nice,' I said. 'And what a pretty name Blanche is – most unusual!'

'After Bill's mother,' Anne said. 'And Robert after my father.'

Beth, having rather abruptly broken off a conversation she had been having with a sharp-faced woman dressed entirely in beige, joined us. She greeted Bill and Anne warmly and went on, 'That was Emma Foxwell of the Coda Press – she keeps on trying to tempt me away from Ralph. It's getting a bit embarrassing.'

'How is the old boy these days?' Bill asked.

Ralph Hastings still managed to keep the family publishing business afloat, in spite of threats of takeovers and mergers from the big firms, largely because a few successful authors like Beth remained loyal to him.

Beth pulled a face. 'Struggling. You know how it is. There's a rumour that this enormous American conglomerate is hovering, but so far he's held on.' She turned to Anne and said, 'How are the children?'

I wondered if anyone ever had a conversation with Anne on any other subject. Surely she must have *some* other interests.

'Oh, they're very well, thank you,' Anne said perfunctorily. 'Bill, we really must go.'

'In a minute,' he said, a trace of irritation in his voice. 'I haven't seen these two – well, Sheila, anyway, for ages. Actually, Sheila, you must be in London sometimes, apart from literary bashes like this. Do give us a ring when you're up here next and come to dinner or something and we can have a real chat. I'll just give you our number – we're ex-directory, obviously – and *do* get in touch, won't you?' He took a card from his pocket and scribbled something on it. 'There you go. Don't forget, now.' He turned to Beth. 'Are you and John going to the Royal Academy thing? Oh good, I'll see you there. Have I got my keys?' He fished in his pocket and produced his car keys. 'Right then, we're on our way.'

'I'm sorry we have to rush off.' Now that she'd managed to detach Bill, Anne's tone was placatory. 'But we did promise Nanny, and the children too–' Her voice died away.

'Of course,' I said. 'We quite understand.'

She gave me a grateful look and I wondered if perhaps her ungracious manner wasn't merely shyness and her appearance – an odd mixture of chic and uncertainty – simply insecurity and doubt about her ability to live up to the rather demanding position she now found herself in.

'It *was* nice to see Bill again after all that time,' I said, when Beth and I were finally sitting peacefully in the small Italian restaurant we usually went to when we met in London. 'Goodness, he's changed since we first knew him! Though I suppose we always knew he'd be successful, even in those early days. He had a sort of – I don't know – a sort of *certainty* about him, if you know what I mean, absolutely determined that he was going to the very top. And he has, I suppose. Still, he still seems like the Bill we knew and loved. You see him fairly often, don't you? What's he like now? Has he changed, as a person, I mean?'

Beth looked thoughtful. 'I don't think so. Still the same old charmer! No, really, he's a lovely person and we're all very fond of him.'

'What about his wife?' I asked. 'Much younger, obviously, and not at all what I expected. Really, well, *gauche!*'

'Yes, he didn't marry for ages – making his way, he used to say – and then it was the usual story. She was his researcher.'

'I see,' I said. 'Still, she does seem a bit,

well, dim and wispy!'

Beth laughed. 'Dim and wispy she may be, but she's also the only daughter of Sir Robert Churchman. You know, the owner of the *Daily Gazette*...'

'Good heavens! I'd never have thought Bill was the sort of person to marry for money!'

'Not marrying for money,' Beth said, 'but, as the old saying goes, marrying where money is. And influence, of course. It certainly gave his career a boost at a critical time.'

'Oh well, I suppose that's what life is like when you're in politics.'

'Actually, Anne's a very nice girl. A bit dim, as you say, but she adores Bill.'

'I suppose so,' I said doubtfully. 'Still, when you think of some of the girlfriends he's had! Do you remember Liza Friedman? *She* went on to be editor of *Vogue*, didn't she? And wasn't there some actress? I seem to remember reading about it in one of the tabloids.'

'He certainly had a taste for smart, go-getting females,' Beth said. 'But honestly, I think it's all worked out quite well and he's perfectly happy. Anyway, enough about Bill. Are *you* perfectly happy?'

I smiled. 'Is anyone? No, as I said before, I'm very lucky. My life's reasonably interesting and reasonably placid – don't you find that *placid* is very important at our age? And Michael's a marvellous son. Yes. Really, really lucky! How about you?'

Beth sighed. 'A bit down at the moment.'

'Is it the children?' I asked. 'You said earlier on–'

'Yes, it's the children.'

'What's the matter?'

Beth picked at the remains of her lasagne with her fork, then pushed the plate to one side and said helplessly, 'I don't know.'

'You don't know?' I echoed.

'It sounds silly,' she said, 'when I put it as baldly as that, but, well, there's something wrong and I can't really discover what it is.'

'Wrong with who? Mark or Helen?'

'Both, I think.'

27

The waiter came over and poured some more wine into our glasses and we sat in silence for a moment.

'I can't be sure,' Beth said. 'They've stopped talking to me, you see.'

'But you used to be so close, such a united family!'

'Yes, we were. But then – oh, you know how it is – things drifted a bit. I had to go to Greece for a while to do some research for a book and John was in the States off and on for about a year. Then Mark got this job in television and moved out to a flat in Notting Hill and Helen went to Cambridge. All that shouldn't have made a difference, other families survive much worse, but I just have the feeling that – well – that the children just don't *like* me any more.'

'Oh, surely not!' I protested. 'You know how young people are, all wrapped up in their own affairs, not so much time for us. It's only natural.'

'No, it's not that, I could understand that.' She shook her head. 'No, when I say they don't like me, it's more than that. I think they actually dislike me.'

'What does John say about all this? Do they dislike him too?'

'No, they're just as affectionate as ever with him. He thinks I'm imagining it.'

'Perhaps you are,' I suggested.

'No,' she said vehemently, 'no, I'm not, I swear it.'

'Have you spoken to them about it?' I asked.

'I've tried, but they've always been evasive. Anyway, I never seem to see them alone. Helen only comes home when John's there – she seems to spend all her vacations with friends – and Mark doesn't come at all. And if I invite Mark to have lunch, or say I'm going to Cambridge to see Helen, they make excuses.'

'And you've no idea?' I said tentatively. 'I mean, there's nothing you might have done – or *they* might have done – that would make them not want to see you?'

'Well,' Beth hesitated for a moment, 'I did

upset Mark. You see, when he moved out it wasn't just to be nearer into London. He's moved in with Fiona Packard.'

'The television producer?'

'Yes.'

'But she must be *years* older than he is!'

'She is, she's got a son at Oxford. And she's not really the sort of woman any mother would care to see her son mixed up with – very hard and career-oriented. So I'm afraid I may have said a few things that didn't go down too well.'

'I see.'

Beth leaned forward. 'But I don't think it was that,' she said earnestly. 'I did try to make things better between us. I didn't apologize exactly, but I wrote and told Mark that I understood that he must live his own life... I thought there was some sort of rapprochement. He wrote me a nice affectionate letter, really his old self – he was always such a loving child – but he still hasn't been to see me or asked me to visit them.'

'And Helen?' I asked.

'As I said, she only ever comes home when John's there.' She gave a little laugh. 'She's always been a Daddy's girl. Otherwise she either goes off somewhere abroad or stays with friends. It's almost as if she's avoiding me.'

'And she hasn't said anything–?'

'No.'

'Have you asked her what's the matter?'

Beth shrugged. 'It sounds ridiculous,' she said, 'but I haven't been able to find the words.'

'What does John say about it all?' I asked.

'He just doesn't see it. He simply says that they're grown up now and have their own lives. I think he was rather shattered about the Fiona thing, but he never said anything, well, not to Mark anyway. And, of course, he's been away such a lot the last few years that I don't think he's really taken in the situation.'

'I'm so sorry,' I said. 'It must be horrible for you. But perhaps things will sort themselves out. In the immortal words of my old daily, it may be just a phrase they're going through.'

Beth smiled. 'It may be. I hope so.'

'And how are you in yourself?' I asked. 'How's the arthritis?'

She grimaced. 'About the same. I know it's not going to get any better, but I'm coping so far. Which reminds me–' She reached into her handbag and produced several small foil-wrapped packages of tablets. 'I keep forgetting to take the wretched things.'

'Goodness,' I said, 'whatever are they all for?'

'Oh, this and that. Hang on, I mustn't get them mixed up.' She extracted tablets from two of the packs and gulped them down with some mineral water. 'There now. Isn't old age ghastly? I positively *rattle* with all these pills!'

'Is it anything serious?' I asked.

'No, not really, just a mixture of things. I suppose we should be grateful that the miracles of modern science can keep us going! Which reminds me, have you seen Jean Fraser lately? Poor soul, she's in a wheelchair now – motor neurone disease, it's dreadfully sad.'

We talked a little of old friends and then I asked, 'How's the new book going?'

She sighed. 'Not very well. I suppose I've got too much on my mind, but I'm having a terrible time getting started. I've got a mass of background stuff from when I went to Greece, but I can't seem to get it assimilated. And there were a few things I didn't do when I was out there. I may have to go back. I stayed with Arnold when I was in Athens, did I tell you?'

'No, really! How is he?'

'Just the same – still as courtly as ever!'

'He does seem to live in another age.'

Arnold Winthrop is another old Oxford friend. He's older than us because he was a youngish don when we were under-graduates. He is a classicist and went to live in Athens about twenty years ago because he said he couldn't bear living in a Britain dominated, as he put it with distaste, by pop culture.

He was attached to the British School in Athens for a time and taught at the university, but, apart from a flying visit to attend the funeral of an aged aunt, he's never been back home. He provides a stopping-off point for his many friends and acquaintances visiting Greece and, as his Greek boyfriend Alex is an excellent cook, there are usually a couple of visitors staying in the large, old-fashioned apartment in Kolonaki.

'Any news?' I asked. Arnold is also a clearing-house for literary gossip.

'Um, let me see – oh yes, Magda and Gerald are splitting up and Olivia had the most furious row with her agent and accused him of having screwed up her last American contract, which is utterly ridiculous because I know for a fact that Random House was very doubtful about her last book and didn't intend to renew. Anyway, she's left him and gone to Phillips,

I think. What else? Peter Frobisher has got the most dreadful writer's block – can't even get started on the second part of that trilogy – which is very unfortunate because he had an enormous advance on all three volumes and he's already spent the lot!'

'Goodness,' I said. 'What fascinating lives you all lead!'

'Well, so could you if you didn't live in that western fastness.'

'No, thank you, I couldn't stand the pace. I'm very well off as I am. Though I must say I do love to hear about it all.'

Beth smiled. 'You always were an observer rather than a doer.'

'Much more comfortable.'

She looked thoughtful for a moment and then she said, 'You're probably right, but it does sound like a recipe for middle age.'

'We are middle-aged, dear,' I reminded her.

'But I don't *feel* it,' she said fiercely. 'Inside I'm still eighteen, still wanting so much out of life!'

'You haven't done too badly already,' I said mildly. 'Most people would say you've had a rich, full life.'

'I know, I've been very fortunate, but I still feel that there's so much more–' She looked at me accusingly. 'I do believe you're *content*. Calm of mind, all passion spent?'

'I wouldn't go that far,' I protested. 'But yes, I probably am contented.'

Beth laughed. 'Good old Sheila,' she said, 'you're a lesson to us all!'

Chapter Two

'Well then,' Michael said, 'are you glad you went?'

'Yes, in a way. The actual thing wasn't really my cup of tea, but it was nice to see Bill North again after all these years, and Beth, too. Though I'm really concerned about her. I don't think she's very well and she's dreadfully worried about her children.'

'It is the natural state for mothers to be worried about their children,' Michael said sententiously.

'Yes, I know *that*, but I mean really worried, not just maternal fretting.'

'I expect they just want to do their own thing and don't want their mother looking over their shoulder all the time.'

'But Beth isn't like that,' I protested. 'She's not a possessive mother, never has been.'

'Well, if Mark's shacked up with this ancient femme fatale, I dare say she did put the pressure on a bit.'

'Well yes, a bit, but she says they sorted all that out. And then there's Helen never going home in the university vacations.'

'I expect she's got other things she wants to do,' Michael said, 'you know how it is.'

'I suppose so. It's just that Beth sounded so – well – *desolated,* really hurt. Oh well, I expect things will sort themselves out.'

But I continued to worry about Beth and her problems and one evening I rang her up. She sounded much more cheerful.

'Lovely to hear from you,' she said. 'It was so nice seeing you – you really must come up and stay for a bit. We didn't talk properly, I never really got your news. As I recall, I was moaning all the time and you hardly got a word in edgeways!'

'I've been worried about you,' I said, 'you seemed so upset about the children. I thought I'd ring and find out how things are going.'

'Bless you, that is kind. Things are about the same, really. Still no real contact with Helen. But I did have a phone call from Mark – much more his old self – to see how we were and to tell me about a new programme he thinks he may be doing for Channel 4. Quite chatty.'

'That sounds *much* better,' I said. 'Perhaps everything will be all right there. I mean, if you can accept the Fiona situation–'

'Oh well, I suppose we'll have to if we want to get Mark's trust back again. No, it was lovely to hear him going on like he used to.'

'Well, it seems to have cheered you up,' I said. 'You sound like a different person!'

'It did help, certainly,' Beth said, 'and then I'm going to Greece next month. I think I told you there's still some stuff I need to research for my new book. I'm really looking forward to that – getting right away from everything for a bit.'

'Well, if you see Arnold, do give him my love.'

'He keeps asking when *you're* going to Athens.'

'Oh, I don't know, foreign travel always seems such a *bother* – trying to remember where I put my passport and getting the currency and waiting about for hours at airports–'

'You *are* getting middle-aged!' Beth exclaimed. 'You really must snap out of it, Sheila.'

'Well, I am middle-aged and I've *been* abroad and things do get too much trouble–'

'You're incorrigible!'

'Anyway,' I said, 'you have a lovely time and try and relax and stop worrying.'

'She seems better,' I told my friend Rosemary the next day, when we were sorting through the garments for the Red Cross Nearly New sale. 'Much more cheerful. She'd heard from Mark – only a telephone call, but I think she felt things were improving on *that* front. Though I think she's still worried about Helen.'

'Girls are always more difficult than boys,' Rosemary said. 'I know I agonized far more over Jilly than I ever did over Martin. The things that go wrong with their lives always seem to be more complicated somehow.'

'Anyway, Beth's going off to Greece quite soon, so that should take her mind off things.'

'Lucky her!' Rosemary said enviously. 'I can't remember *when* Jack and I went away last – oh yes, I do! It was that disastrous weekend we spent with his sister Christine in Aberdovey! It poured all the time and Christine and Leslie made us play bridge, and you know how bad I am and Jack's not much better – though he thinks he is – and overbids quite dreadfully all the time and gets so bad tempered. It was absolutely ghastly!'

'I don't expect Beth will be playing bridge in Greece,' I said.

'No.' Rosemary sighed. 'Greece certainly seems more exciting than North Wales. But you know I've never been able to get Jack to go abroad. Well, we did go to Paris that time, but he got food poisoning the second day we were there and that was that!'

'Poor Rosemary,' I said, laughing. 'Do you yearn for glamorous foreign climes?'

'Well, it wouldn't do me much good if I did. Anyway, I couldn't leave Mother, and then there are the animals–'

'I know,' I said. 'Beth's very lucky – no responsibilities any more, not to mention all that lovely money to smooth away any difficulties that might arise!'

'Oh well,' Rosemary said philosophically, 'it takes all sorts, I suppose. I don't think I'd rather be anyone but me. Would you?'

'Not really. I mean, I'd like Peter to still be here, but otherwise I don't think I'd want to change anything else.'

'Oh, for goodness' sake!' Rosemary held up a crumpled polyester skirt in a particularly hideous shade of blue. 'I don't call *this* nearly new, do you? People really are extraordinary!'

What with the Red Cross sale and then Michael going off on a course, and needing a great deal of washing, ironing and packing to be done for him, I didn't give much more thought to Beth and her problems. While Michael was away one evening, I was sitting, half-dozing in front of a gardening programme on the television, with Foss on my lap and the two dogs trying to edge me off the sofa, when the telephone rang.

'Oh, Sheila, it's John – John Blackmore.'

He broke off and there was a moment's silence and I said, 'John? Are you there? What's the matter?'

'I'm sorry, Sheila–' His voice was husky, as if he had trouble speaking. 'I'm sorry, but I wanted you to hear before it was in the papers.'

He broke off again and I said urgently, 'John, what is it? What's the matter?'

'It's Beth – she's dead.'

'No! Oh, John, no! What happened?'

'Some sort of ghastly accident – a mix-up

with her pills – I don't know. They don't seem to know yet *what* it was.'

'Oh, John, I'm so sorry. Where ... I mean, where did it happen? Was it at home? Were you there?'

'No, she was at the cottage. She said she wanted to get all her notes and things together before she went to Greece.' The Blackmores had a cottage in the Cotswolds which they used for weekends and where Beth quite often went to work. 'I was in London. Mrs Moss, our daily, found her this morning. She called the doctor, but it was too late.'

'How dreadful–'

'If only I'd been there!' John burst out. 'It would never have happened!'

'You mustn't blame yourself,' I said urgently. 'You have to be strong for the children. How are they?'

'Stunned, I suppose. I don't think it's really sunk in yet. Helen's coming up from Cambridge today. Mark, poor boy, broke down on the telephone. He couldn't talk. I'll ring him tomorrow.'

'And how about you, John?' I asked. 'Is there anyone with you?'

'No. Helen will be here soon, though. I've only just got back to Kew – I've been at the cottage most of the day. There's got to be an inquest, apparently. It's all so confusing. Honestly, Sheila, I can't believe she's gone!' His voice broke.

'Is there anything I can do? Anything at all? Would you like me to ring people?'

'No, that's all right. I've phoned Bill and Anne and Ralph, of course. Oh yes, if you could get in touch with Arnold. She was going to stay with him in Athens – I expect she told you. Do you have a number for him?'

'Yes, I have. I'll do that straight away.'

'Thank you, Sheila, that would be kind.'

I hesitated for a moment, then, 'What about the funeral?' I asked tentatively.

'We don't know if there's got to be a post-mortem, the doctor down there wasn't sure. But whenever the funeral is, it will be just the children and me. Oh, and Beth's brother, Andrew, he'll be coming down from Scotland. Ralph seems to think there ought to be some sort of memorial service. I don't know–'

'Don't worry about that now,' I said. 'John, have you had anything to eat?'

'Eat? No, I don't think I have.'

'Well, do try and have something, even if it's only a sandwich. You could make one for Helen, too. She'll want something after her journey.'

'Yes – yes, she will. Thank you, Sheila, I'll do that.'

'Take care of yourself,' I said. 'I'll be in touch. Please give my love to the children and, John, I'm so very sorry.'

When I had put the telephone down I sat quietly for a moment, still unable to take in what I had heard. Tris, sensing my distress, came and pawed at my knee, whining a little. Mechanically I stroked his white head and cried a little for my friend.

After a while I got up and rang Arnold.

'Beth? Dead? it's impossible!'

'I'm sorry, Arnold, but I'm afraid it's true.'

'But she was coming here, to stay with us–'

'I know, it's awful.'

'What happened?'

I told him what John had said and added, 'I don't know how he'll cope without her, they were so devoted. And there are the children... We're all going to miss her very much.'

'Yes – I can't imagine a world without Beth. Excuse me, Sheila, I can't talk any more. I'll write to you. Goodbye.'

There was an item about Beth on the radio news that evening and obituaries in all the major newspapers. None of them, though, seemed to be about the Beth I knew – just a brief biography, lists of her books, critical evaluations of them and pompous pronouncements about Dame Elizabeth Blackmore's place in the mainstream of English literature. There was nothing there of the Beth with whom I had shared part of my youth, agonized over love affairs, laughed about the absurdities of life and chatted endlessly and pleasurably about nothing in particular in the way real friends do.

A few days later I found Bill North's card in my handbag and rang him. Anne answered the phone.

'Oh hello, this is Sheila Malory. I don't suppose you remember me – we met at that Writer of the Year thing–'

'Oh yes,' the quiet voice said cautiously. 'Yes, I remember meeting you.'

'I wonder if I could speak to Bill?'

'He's at the House, I'm afraid.'

'Oh. Stupid of me, I should have thought. It's just that I wanted to have a word about Beth.'

'Yes, of course, I'll tell him when he comes in. He'll ring you then, if it's not too late.' There was a moment's pause and she went on, 'I was so sorry to hear about her death. Such a shocking thing to have happened. The family must be dreadfully upset.'

The banal phrases irritated me – though, goodness knows, what else *could* she have said? – so I said quite briskly, 'Yes, well, thank you very much. I'll look forward to hearing from Bill,' and put the phone down.

Then I felt rather mean, because, after all, how could she be expected to share our particular kind of sorrow? She had only known Beth briefly and superficially, they weren't part of each other's lives. I suppose, subconsciously, I resented the fact that she, a pale nonentity, was alive and Beth, clever, funny, complicated Beth, was not.

Bill rang quite late. I'd already shut the animals up for the night and was about to go upstairs.

'Sheila? Sorry to ring at this hour – a late-night sitting. Isn't it damnable about Beth?'

'I still can't believe it,' I said. 'Bill, I hope you didn't mind me ringing. It's just that I wanted to talk to someone who – well – who remembers.'

'Yes, I know. It all comes back, doesn't it?'

'Mostly the good times, the fun–'

'God, yes! We were so lucky. I think we were the last generation who really got a kick out of Oxford. We *enjoyed* it all so much, and without drugs too!'

I laughed. 'A certain amount of drink, though.'

'A certain amount. True. Mind you, Beth hardly drank at all; nor did you, for that matter.'

'Girls didn't then,' I said. 'It was how we were brought up. But we didn't seem to need drink – just being at Oxford was exciting enough. In spite of all the restrictions, like being in by twelve. Do you remember, after that OUDS party, Jeremy got us that punt from Magdalen and took it down-river to St Hilda's and then Beth and I climbed in through the buttery window, which Megan had left open for us, only to come face to face with the bursar, making herself a nice hot drink!'

'Young people today don't know what they're missing!' Bill said. 'All this freedom – boring!'

'It seems a long time ago,' I said sadly. 'Beth is the first of our year to go. I gather it was an accident. John said there was some sort of mix-up with her pills. He didn't go into details and I couldn't ask. Do you know any more?'

'Not really. It all seems such a bloody awful waste!' he burst out. 'Such a stupid way to die!'

'I know. She'd been very depressed about the children, I was really quite worried about her. But when I phoned her about ten days ago she was really happy. She was going to Greece, did she tell you? And that seemed to have cheered her up no end.'

'Yes, she was looking forward to it.'

'And I think the new book was starting to come together and she was quite excited about doing the research,' I said. 'Oh, it's heartbreaking to think of it! I rang Arnold – John asked me to – and he was shattered. I've always thought that he was a little in love with Beth.'

'Yes, I believe you're right. I think Alex

was always a bit edgy when Beth was in Athens – jealous, I expect.'

'Poor Arnold. I must write to him. John said it would be a family-only funeral, but Ralph wants a memorial service.'

'People would expect one, certainly. Will you go?'

'Oh, yes.'

'Have lunch with me afterwards?'

'Yes, thank you, Bill. I'd like to do that.'

As I put the phone down and moved into the hall, the dogs, hearing that I was still up, began to bark. On an impulse I let them and Foss out of the kitchen.

'Come on,' I said. 'You can come and sleep upstairs tonight.'

They all rushed up the stairs ahead of me and I followed more slowly, obscurely comforted.

Chapter Three

I can't see why people make a lot of fuss about ironing. Actually, I quite like it. I enjoy seeing the creases and wrinkles give way to nice smooth fabric and I find the warm smell of freshly washed and ironed clothes rather cosy. I usually have the radio on, though sometimes I plan the opening of a rather tricky review I'm working on or, simply, move the iron around without thinking of anything at all, enjoying the sheer mindlessness of the exercise. This particular day I was listening to a rather tiresome young man interviewing people in Tennessee as he travelled down the Natchez Trace Trail. I was struck by their politeness and good humour as they answered his fatuous and patronizing questions and marvelled again at the good manners of most Americans.

The telephone startled me and when I heard John's voice it took me a moment to take in what he was saying.

'We've just had news of Beth's will. We more or less knew what was in it, but she'd added a codicil quite recently, while I was away. I suppose that's why I didn't know about it.' He paused for a moment and then said, 'Sheila, Beth appointed you to be her literary executor.'

'Me?'

'Yes. Hadn't she asked if you'd be willing?'

'No,' I said. 'She never mentioned it.'

'Oh.' John sounded surprised. 'Well, it was just before ... before she died. I expect she was going to talk to you about it. You will do it?'

'Yes, of course I will.'

'That's good of you, Sheila,' he said warmly.

'I'm not sure what it involves—'

'Perhaps you could have a word with Ralph, he'll know what needs to be done.

Do you know him?'

'I think I met him once,' I said. 'Ages ago, at some literary do.'

'I'll ask him to get in touch with you. I'm very grateful.'

'I can't think why Beth wanted me, though.'

'You were her friend,' John said, 'and she valued your judgement.'

'Well, I'll do the best I can,' I said, 'if that's what Beth wanted.'

'There's another thing. She left you a small legacy – £10,000 and her pearl necklace.'

'Oh no!' I protested. 'I couldn't!'

'I expect the money's a small thank you for being her literary executor,' John said. 'And she would have wanted you to have the necklace, as a memento.'

'But Helen should have it.'

'She has the other jewellery. At least, Beth left it to her, but Helen says she doesn't want it, won't have it.'

'But why?'

John sighed. 'I really don't know. Honestly, Sheila, she's been behaving very strangely.'

'I expect she's upset,' I said.

'No – at least, I don't think so. She doesn't seem to be grieving for her mother at all. She only seems upset at *my* grief, if you see what I mean.'

'She's very young,' I said gently, 'and the young often find it difficult to express their feelings.'

'You're probably right. I suppose I'm just finding it difficult to cope with anything at the moment.'

'How about Mark?' I asked tentatively.

'Now he *was* upset,' John said. 'In tears, poor boy – it hit him very hard.'

'Have you seen him?'

'No, we've spoken several times on the phone. I'll see him at the funeral, of course. Whenever that may be. The inquest's on Friday. I must say I'll be glad when it's all over. All this dragging things out makes things ten times worse.'

'Poor John, I'm so sorry. It must be horrible for you all.'

'If we could just have the funeral!' he burst out. 'Get it over. This being in limbo's so hard. The children need to get on with their lives.'

'And you, too.'

'Yes. Perhaps when she's laid to rest I shall really accept that it's happened and I'll never see her again.'

'Literary executor!' Michael said. 'That sounds very grand. Or is it one of those literary thankless tasks, like doing an index or something?'

'Honestly, I haven't the faintest idea *what's* involved,' I said. 'I'll just have to wait until I hear from Ralph Hastings.'

'He's Beth's publisher?'

'Yes. And a very old friend. He'll miss her dreadfully. Actually, he'll miss her professionally too. Beth was one of his most successful authors. I should think he can ill afford to lose her.'

I looked with some misgiving at the plastic bag Michael had brought into the kitchen.

'What's in that?' I asked cautiously.

'A couple of rabbits Jonah gave me for the animals.'

'Oh. How kind of him.'

Michael laughed. 'It's all right, Ma, I'll see to them. Just keep out of the kitchen for half an hour while I skin them and cut them up.'

I expressed my gratitude, though my heart sank at the thought of the way the smell of boiling rabbit pervades the whole house and at the horrid task of taking out the millions of little sharp bones while the animals, frantic to get at the end product, whined and scratched at the door.

I had a letter from Ralph Hastings the following week, asking me to have lunch when I was next in London.

'I think I'll go up on Tuesday,' I said to Michael. 'Just for the day. I'd quite like to have a quick whizz round the Whistler exhibition at the Tate, so I could kill two birds with one stone.'

Ralph Hastings asked me to meet him at the Ivy, a restaurant I hadn't been to for years – not, in fact, since Peter and I, eager young theatregoers in the 1970s, used to go for a special treat to gaze at the theatrical luminaries who were to be seen there.

As usual, I was far too early and wandered up and down Charing Cross Road looking at the secondhand bookshops. I'd just stopped to take my hand mirror out to check that my hair wasn't too blown about when I saw a tall figure that I recognized turning down West Street. I dragged a comb quickly through my hair and followed him.

The Ivy was quite different from how I remembered it. I felt slightly melancholy to see how the old shabbiness had been replaced by a brisk new elegance.

Ralph Hastings stood up politely when he saw me.

'Mrs Malory, how very good of you to spare the time to see me.'

We shook hands and, while we were

studying the menu, I glanced at him surreptitiously. His appearance was familiar to me from the society pages of the glossy magazines I flipped through under the dryer at the hairdresser – tall and very distinguished, with thick grey hair and the sort of expensive tan it is only possible to achieve abroad.

'Well now,' he said, 'what shall we have? Shall we start with the crostini and grilled vegetables?'

'That sounds very nice,' I said meekly.

'And to follow, I can recommend the fricassée of wild rabbit with porcini mushrooms.'

I shuddered at the memory of boiling rabbit and said, 'I think I'd like the monkfish. It's always nice to have things you can't have at home.'

He smiled as if I'd said something amusing.

'A splendid choice. I'll have the same.'

While he and the waiter embarked on a detailed discussion of the wine list, I surveyed the room, looking hopefully for a celebrity I could tell Rosemary about, but apart from a minor television interviewer talking to an actor whose face I knew but whose name escaped me, there was no one I recognized.

The waiter withdrew and Ralph Hastings turned the full force of his attention back to me. He was, I felt, a somewhat overwhelming character, full of energy and a kind of restrained power, the sort of person who always makes me feel inadequate.

'I just can't believe Beth has gone,' he said. 'It was a terrible blow when I heard. She had so much marvellous work still before her–'

'It's dreadful,' I agreed.

'And to go in such a way,' he went on.

'I still don't know the details,' I said. 'John simply said there'd been a mix-up with the tablets, but I don't know what–'

'Beth was taking some sort of digitalis-based tablets for a heart condition and then there was the arthritis.'

'I knew about the arthritis,' I said in surprise, 'but I didn't know there was anything wrong with her heart!'

'No, well, that was fairly recent and she didn't like talking about it. You know how dismissive she always was about illness.'

I remembered Beth's casual reference to 'this and that' at our last meeting. 'Yes,' I said.

'Well, apparently the ibuprofen she took for the arthritis shouldn't be taken with the digitalis. I suppose she got muddled somehow and took them at the wrong time, in the wrong order. I don't know the details. Anyway, that's what killed her – so stupid! Such a silly way to die!'

'Good God,' I said, 'that's dreadful! How could it have happened? It seemed to me that she was so careful about taking her tablets. No wonder John was so upset. If he'd been there it might not have happened!'

'I know. He blames himself, but that's ridiculous. It just happened, no one's fault.'

'Poor John,' I said, 'poor Beth.'

We were both silent for a moment.

'So,' Ralph said, 'Beth made you her literary executor.'

'Yes. It was a complete surprise – I'd no idea. Apparently it was a recent codicil to her will.'

'I know she admired your work.' He gave me a charming smile. 'I imagine she wanted you to be the one who would write her official biography.'

'But it's very peculiar,' I said. 'I mean, we're almost the same age – actually, she's a few months younger than I am – so I might quite easily have died before she did.'

'Well, maybe the heart thing made her more aware of her own mortality.'

'Yes, perhaps it did.'

I was silent while I wrestled surreptitiously with my very crisp crostini. Then I said tentatively, 'Actually, I'm not really sure what's involved in being a literary executor.'

'I imagine John will hold the copyright on her works,' Ralph said, suddenly very businesslike. 'So it will be mostly a question of going through her papers – unpublished manuscripts and so on – and seeing if anything can be done with them. Then you'll have to see any further editions of her work through the press. Actually I had planned a new uniform edition, so that will have to be set in hand. I believe she wanted her manuscripts and papers to go to the Senate House Library at London University – she used to say that the Bodleian always got the plums – and I believe she knows the deputy librarian there.'

'Oh yes, of course, Janet Williams! We were all at Oxford together.'

'Yes, well, you'll have to arrange that. And then there'll be the research students wanting help with their theses.'

'Oh, goodness!'

'There have been several studies of her work, as you probably know, and now there will be many more.'

'An absolute gift to Ph.D. students,' I said, 'looking for someone who hasn't been "done" already – all those Jake Balokov-skys!'

'I'm afraid so. Though, as I said, I imagine you'll do the official biography. I wonder,' he said thoughtfully, 'if there are sufficient letters to make a separate volume.'

'I think I'll wait and see what John wants,' I said.

'Oh yes, of course.'

'It all sounds a bit formidable,' I said.

'It's very time-consuming, and expensive too.'

'Expensive?'

'I remember Rebecca West's literary executor telling me that the postage involved was horrendous, especially to America.'

'That won't be a problem. Beth very kindly left me £10,000.'

'That's good. Now then, will you have a pudding? They do a superlative treacle tart.'

'No really, I couldn't.'

'Coffee, then? Right. Well, Sheila – I hope I may call you Sheila – I will look forward very much to working with you. Please, contact me if there's *any* sort of problem. What I want – and I'm sure you want it too – is to keep Beth's name where it should be (where, indeed, it has always been), in the forefront of the literary scene. She is, after all, one of the greatest novelists of our time and I would hate to think that her work might be forgotten.' He leaned forward to make his point more forcefully. 'It is up to us, Sheila, to keep her work alive and before the public. I look upon it as a sacred trust and I'm sure you feel the same.'

Slightly taken aback at the magnitude of the task he appeared to be laying upon me, I murmured that I would do my best.

'Excellent, excellent. Now, may I pour you a little more wine?'

'It all sounds very glamorous,' Rosemary said.

'It *was* nice,' I replied, 'having a treat like that and seeing how the other half lives.'

'So what's involved in this executor business?'

'Oh, sorting out the papers, seeing things through the press, that sort of thing. And I think I have to give permission to people who want to quote from the books or manuscripts. I shall know more when I've been up to London again and seen how the land lies. John said he's brought all the papers back to Kew from the cottage. Actually, I think he wants to sell the cottage – too many unhappy associations.'

'It sounds to me', Rosemary said thoughtfully, 'as if it's going to take up a lot of your time.'

'Yes, I expect it will.'

'You could bring some of the papers back here and work on them at home.'

'I suppose I might, though I don't know what the form is. Beth wanted her papers to go to the Senate House Library in London, so I may have to work on them there. I'm going up next week to see what I have to do.'

'Where will you stay?'

'John did invite me to stay at Kew, but I don't think I want to do that. No, I thought I'd go and stay with Cousin Hilda.'

'Goodness!' Rosemary exclaimed. 'You *are* brave!'

My cousin Hilda is, indeed, a formidable person, holding firm opinions expressed with extreme forthrightness. She is the only child of my father's elder brother and so considerably older than me. For many years I was absolutely terrified of her. But I have found that, underneath an apparently unbending exterior, there is great kindness and a great understanding of the human condition. With advancing years (and maturity) I have come to appreciate both her caustic wit and her wisdom.

She has never married, expending her considerable energy on her career. During the war she was at Bletchley Park, working on the code-breaking programme, and after the war she rose through the ranks of the higher Civil Service to become one of the first women Assistant Secretaries. Since her retirement she has sat on various government committees (arousing fear and admiration in equal measure in her fellow members) and has wrested the financial reins of the parish from her local vicar, to his mingled relief and resentment. Although I am convinced that she regards me as frivolous and lacking a properly serious attitude to life, she has always treated me with great kindness and has been, in moments of real crisis an absolute rock. Also, she is devoted to Michael.

I rang her that evening to ask if I could come to stay.

'That would be delightful, Sheila. As a matter of fact, I was about to telephone you to ask your advice.'

'*My* advice?' I asked incredulously. 'What about?'

'Since you are coming here shortly it will be simpler if I explain the nature of the problem when I see you. So, you will be arriving on Monday, just after noon, you said?'

The telephone clicked and she was gone, leaving me seething with curiosity.

'What can it be?' I asked Michael. 'I mean, she's always regarded me as an amiable fool, so what on earth can she want my advice about?'

'The possibilities are so obscure that I will not even begin to hazard a guess,' he replied. 'You will just have to possess your soul in patience until next Monday.'

Chapter Four

My cousin Hilda had the good fortune – or it might have been the foresight – to buy a small mews house in Holland Park just after the war, when property prices were very low indeed. I imagine it must be worth a small fortune today. As my taxi drew up at the entrance to the mews, I savoured the peace and quiet – a small oasis in the middle of the traffic rushing madly from Kensington to Hammersmith.

Hilda greeted me rather oddly, I thought. She held the door open only a crack and said hurriedly, 'Come in quickly!' As I went in, she shut the door smartly behind me.

'I'm sorry about that,' she said, 'but I don't want him to go out before you've seen him.'

I looked at her in bewilderment.

'Him?' I asked.

'Yes. Come into the sitting-room, I think he's there, though he may have gone up-stairs–'

She led the way into the small sitting-room and I followed cautiously, wondering who on earth I was going to meet.

'Oh, *there* he is!' Hilda exclaimed. 'Tolly, come and meet Sheila.'

Sitting on the windowsill, to the imminent danger of several potted plants, was a half-grown Siamese cat. As I came into the room, he leaped down and, winding himself round my legs, uttered a loud cry, presumably of greeting.

I bent to pick him up and as I stroked him he purred loudly and complacently.

'What did you say his name was?'

'Tolly, short for Ptolemy.'

'But whose is he?' I asked.

'Mine.'

I looked at Hilda in amazement. She has never been what is known as an animal lover, indeed she has often commented with some acerbity about the habits of my animals and the 'ridiculous' (I quote her) way I indulge them. She shifted in some embarrassment before my astonished gaze.

'It's a long story,' she said. 'You remember my friend Agnes Waterfield?'

'Yes, yes, I do.'

'She had him as a kitten – she always kept cats, you may remember. But then her eldest son, who lives in Australia, had a car accident and was left virtually crippled. He had no one to look after him, so she had to go. She didn't feel she could take Tolly – she thought she would have quite enough on her hands – so she asked me to take him. I refused, of course, but she was so insistent and so upset about her son that I felt, in the end, that I had to agree.'

'Good gracious!' I said. 'How long have you had him?'

'Just on three weeks. So you can see how providential it is that you should come and stay because there are so many things I need to know about looking after him properly.'

'Yes, well–'

I was at a loss, finding it almost impossible to accept the juxtaposition of my austere cousin and a potentially wild Siamese.

'He's a chocolate-point, you know,' she said with pride, 'and a very fine specimen. Do you know, he's got three champions and *four* supreme champions in his pedigree. I'll show it to you after lunch.'

At the word, Tolly jumped down from my lap and leaped on to Hilda's. She smiled lovingly at him. 'Who's Mummy's clever boy, then? *Wasn't* that clever of him to know when I mentioned food! Come along, lunch is quite ready. I'll just give Tolly his first–' She got up and put the cat on her shoulder, where he gazed at me smugly as I followed her into the kitchen.

I rang John and arranged to go to Kew the next day. The Blackmores live in one of those very desirable eighteenth-century houses on Kew Green and John led me down into the basement, where Beth had a study.

'I haven't been through the desk yet,' he said, 'so I don't know what's there, apart from personal stuff, of course, but those boxes there are full of manuscripts. I haven't really looked at them. I thought I'd leave all that to you.' He indicated about a dozen large cardboard boxes stacked against one wall. 'There's still a bit more at the cottage, I couldn't get it all in the car. Still, I expect there's enough there for you to be getting on with.'

'Yes,' I said, rather overwhelmed at the prospect of sorting through such a mass of material. 'I'd better get started.'

'Well, come and have a cup of coffee first,' John said. 'I've got some made.'

We sat in the kitchen, a charming room looking out on to a small walled garden, thickly planted with shrubs and climbing plants and with a small fountain at the far end.

'How are the children?' I asked.

He shrugged. 'I can't really make them out. Mark is really upset, absolutely devastated, I could tell that when I spoke to him on the phone, but he didn't come to the funeral. That woman – Fiona – rang up to say that he was too ill.'

'And Helen?'

'Helen's been marvellous, really supportive. She stayed with me all the way through, after the funeral as well. In fact, she only went back to Cambridge yesterday. But–'

'But what?'

'It's most peculiar. She simply won't talk about her mother. Whenever I tried to say something she just changed the subject.'

'You must give her time,' I said. 'Things will sort themselves out.'

'Yes. It's better now we've got the inquest out of the way.'

'How was it?'

'Just a formality, really. Death by misadventure, the coroner's sympathy – all quite brief, thank God.'

'How about you? Are you coping?'

'Oh well, you know how it is.'

'Yes,' I said. 'I know.'

He looked at me and said, 'Oh God, Sheila, how awful of me. Of *course* you know how it is – you lost Peter–'

'Yes, but it's worse for you, somehow. I mean, I knew that Peter was dying, but with Beth it was so sudden, so unexpected. But, yes, I do know how you feel and what a terrible gap there is in your life. It will get better, believe me, but it takes time and I won't pretend that it isn't hellish. Still, you have your work, that's a great help.'

'Yes, I suppose so. Actually, I have to go to Düsseldorf next week. Look, I'll give you a key so that you can come and go here while I'm away. Mrs Havers, our daily, comes in every day – she should be here soon, so I'll introduce you – but otherwise you'll have the place to yourself if you want to get things sorted.'

For the next few days I tried to classify Beth's papers. They were mostly manuscripts, some of books already published, but there were quite a few unpublished short stories and what looked like several novels or parts of novels. There was also a pile of the notebooks in which Beth used to jot down ideas for characters and plots, as well as scraps of dialogue and incidents she had come across or overheard.

I telephoned Ralph and told him what I had found.

'The short stories sound good,' he said. 'Will there be enough for a volume?'

'I think so,' I replied cautiously, 'though I haven't read them yet, so I don't know if they'd all be suitable.'

'And what about the novels?'

'A couple of them look like juvenilia,' I said. 'Not for publication. I don't know about the others. One of them isn't finished, so I imagine it was something she tried and abandoned.'

'But the other?' he asked eagerly.

'I really couldn't say until I've read it.'

'A new novel by Beth Blackmore would have tremendous publicity value,' he said.

'I'm sure it would,' I replied, 'but only if it's up to her own high standard. I couldn't agree to anything else and I'm sure John would feel the same.'

'Of course,' Ralph agreed hastily. 'But you must admit it would be a great pity if her public was denied one last book, one more Elizabeth Blackmore.'

'Yes, well, I'm going back to Taviscombe for a few days and I'll take some of the stuff with me and read it there, then I'll be able to let you know more definitely what is and what isn't suitable.'

'That would be quite excellent,' he said smoothly. 'I have every faith in your judgement.'

'I know he's desperate to cash in on Beth's name,' I said to Michael, 'but I really don't want just *anything* published. Beth would hate that, she was so meticulous about her work, such a perfectionist. I couldn't bear her work to be exploited.'

'Well,' Michael said judiciously, 'that's

what you're there for, that's what being a literary executor is all about, isn't it? Don't let Ralph Hastings bounce you into agreeing to anything you think is unsuitable.'

'No,' I said, 'you're absolutely right! Mind you, he is pretty formidable. I hope I can stand up to him'

Michael smiled. 'You will, Ma. I know what you're like when you dig your heels in! So, tell me more about Cousin Hilda.'

I poured myself another glass of sherry. 'Well, you simply wouldn't believe the change. She's positively *soppy* about that little cat, absolutely dotes!'

'But she's always been so disapproving about Foss, complaining about him sitting on chairs and saying how unhygienic it is for him to jump up on the worktop.'

'Ptolemy sleeps on her bed.'

'No!'

'Yes, *and* the bath is covered in black pawmarks and when he sits in the sink and tries to drink from the tap she positively coos over him and says how clever he is.'

'Oh well, the end of the world is definitely at hand and I fully expect to see a whole squadron of pigs flying over the Bristol Channel!'

I read Beth's novel very carefully. Although it was obviously unrevised, it was very powerfully written, more simple and forthright than her usual more delicate and allusive style and had none of the philosophical undertones that gave Beth's work its depth and complexity. It was about a rich industrialist, a man of great power and influence, brought down by his obsessive love for an unsuitable woman. She was plain and eccentric, but immensely charismatic and his equal in strength and determination and the ascendency she gradually gained over him finally destroyed him.

As I finished the book and laid it aside I was, quite frankly, dismayed. It was a remarkable book by any standard, but I wasn't at all sure what should be done with it. If Ralph Hastings had been expecting 'one more Elizabeth Blackmore', he would be disappointed. And what would Beth have wanted? This was so unlike her usual style, so raw and somehow personal, as her other books had never been. I was sure that she wouldn't have wanted it published. No, I would tell Ralph that it was not in a finished enough state for publication and he could make do with the volume of short stories. These were much more typical and, although Beth always said that the short story wasn't really her medium, it seemed to me that she had succeeded very well. Some of the stories were rather slight, but one or two had the sharp perception and depth of understanding that characterized her best work.

But, as I was hastily throwing together a ginger cake for the St John's Ambulance Bring and Buy sale, my thoughts kept returning to the novel. What had prompted her to write it? Was she simply experimenting, trying something new? Or was there a more personal reason behind it? Certainly I sensed the sort of immediacy in the writing that often comes with an intense personal involvement, but for the life of me I couldn't think what there was in her own life that might have inspired it. The fact that the main protagonist was a businessman suggested that there was some connection with John, but the character was so totally unlike John – or, least, the John I knew – that I dismissed that theory as impossible. Perhaps, I thought, there could be a clue in one of the notebooks, where she might have jotted down some sort of notes or rough outline.

That reminded me that I hadn't yet got in touch with Janet Williams. Putting the cake in the oven and setting the timer, I rang the number of the Senate House Library. Her secretary told me that she was away on a course, but made an appointment for me to see her the following week.

'So, I'm afraid,' I said to Rosemary as I delivered the cake, 'I'm going to have to go up to London again next week.'

'Oh well, at least you'll be here for the Bring and Buy, thank goodness for that!' Rosemary said fervently. 'There's absolutely *no one* else to do the produce stall. People have simply melted away this time, so who's going to do the teas I really don't know. I suppose I'll have to ask Maureen *again* and I know she's got all her grandchildren staying—'

I had also arranged to see Ralph Hastings, this time at his office, and I wasn't looking forward to the meeting, being unsure of my ability to stand firm, to do what I felt Beth would have wanted, in the face of his persuasion.

Unlike many of the larger publishers, Ralph had kept his offices in Bloomsbury rather than moving out to bigger but less expensive premises in the Fulham hinterland. They were housed in a charming eighteenth-century house just off Bedford Square and Ralph's own office was everything an old-fashioned publisher's office should be, panelled, book-lined, richly appointed in the best possible taste. I gave a little sigh of satisfaction at its perfection as a charming girl assistant ushered me in.

Ralph rose and greeted me warmly.

'Sheila, how good of you to come. Samantha, could you very kindly bring us some coffee?'

The coffee, when it arrived, was in delicate white and gold china and accompanied by delicious *langue de chat* biscuits. I hoped that Ralph's business was as rich as his lifestyle. We discussed the short stories for a while and I arranged to do a little mild editing of some of them before I sent them on to Ralph.

'That will be splendid,' he said. 'We must come to some suitable financial arrangement. With John, too, of course, since he holds the copyright. Perhaps your agent could get in touch with me?'

'I don't have an agent,' I replied. 'I publish so little and usually with one of the university presses.'

'Yes, of course, I quite understand. Then perhaps your son, who is, I believe, a solicitor, could cast his eye over any contract we might have drawn up.'

'Yes, I'm sure that would be fine.'

There was a slightly embarrassed (on my side at least) pause while we both drank our coffee and I accepted another biscuit.

'Now then,' Ralph said, 'what about the novel?'

'No,' I said. 'No, it's not suitable for publication.'

'You mean it isn't finished?'

'Well, it *is* finished – at least, the story is complete, as it were – it's just that the whole thing is so, well, so raw and unpolished. It's quite unlike anything else she's ever written.'

His eyes lit up. 'Really! How interesting. Would you say that she was experimenting with another style, a totally different kind of book? That would be very exciting.'

'No,' I protested. 'At least, I don't think

that's what she was doing. It seems, well, much more *personal* than anything she'd done before. I somehow got the feeling that she'd written it for herself, not for publication.'

Ralph laughed. 'No writer, my dear Sheila, ever writes anything *not* for publication.'

'That may be so,' I said obstinately, 'but I would be very unhappy to see this particular work published. I don't think it would do her reputation any good at all, and, really, that's my main concern.'

'But of course!' His manner was immediately emollient. 'That is what we all want.'

I made no reply and he went on, 'What does John say about all this?'

'I haven't shown him the book yet. He seemed to want to leave all that side of things to me.'

'Very wise, very wise. We all have absolute faith in your judgement, of course. That, after all, is why Beth chose you to be her literary executor, is it not?'

I gave him a perfunctory smile in recognition of the implied compliment. 'Nevertheless,' he continued, 'I would very much like to cast my eye over the manuscript, out of interest. Anything written by Beth is naturally of great interest to us all. And, if, as you say, it is in quite a new vein, well–'

'Yes, of course,' I said formally. 'I'll have a photocopy made to send you.'

His eyebrows rose fractionally at this, but he smiled and said, 'That would be most kind. Meanwhile, perhaps you could persuade John to have a look at it, too – just in case–'

'He's abroad at the moment,' I said, 'but naturally I'll be consulting him. Actually, I rather want to get all the papers moved to the Senate House Library as soon as possible. John's already passed on to me letters from several scholars who want to look at them and obviously they can't do that at Kew.'

He looked thoughtful. 'Yes, there will be

quite a race to see who can bring out the first study. You will, of course, want to refuse any rights to use of the unpublished material until you have completed your own biography.'

'Oh dear, do I have to? It seems rather mean.'

'It is usual. You can give access to the papers as long as nothing is directly quoted.'

'Actually,' I said, rather taken aback by all this, 'I haven't really thought about writing Beth's biography. I mean, I'd like to, of course, but I don't know if–'

'My dear Sheila,' Ralph said smoothly, 'there is no one more fitting than you. Besides, I am sure you would rather write it yourself than have someone of a different generation, from a different country or culture, even, making all the wrong assumptions about Beth's life and work.'

'Well, if you put it like that–'

'And I very much hope that you will give me the honour of publishing it. I thought it would be most suitable if it appeared in the same series, as it were, as the new uniform edition of Beth's novels that I have already set in hand.'

'So,' I said to Hilda that evening, 'it looks as if I'm going to be very busy for the next six months – longer, really, because I expect writing a life of someone you actually knew is much more difficult than doing that of some figure in the distant literary past. Are you sure you don't mind me staying here? I'll share expenses, of course–'

'My dear Sheila, as I told you before, I shall be delighted. Already you have been most helpful about Tolly's injections and the flea collar, and,' she added, with just a hint of jealousy, looking at Tolly peaceful, for once, on my knee, 'he does seem to have taken to you quite remarkably.'

'Oh, I expect he can smell Foss on my skirt,' I said placatingly.

Tolly, hearing his name, opened one bright blue eye, purred very loudly and composed himself once more to sleep.

'I expect he's tired,' Hilda said. 'He was out in the gardens at the back of the mews all day. Did I tell you,' she asked, her voice softening with pride, 'he brought a mouse in!'

'Really?'

'Yes. Actually, it wasn't a mouse but a little shrew and it wasn't dead, so when he opened his mouth to tell me what a clever boy he'd been, it got away. It ran behind that bookcase over there. I couldn't get it out, of course, and he was *very* cross with me and do you know he sat by the bookcase for a full half-hour waiting for the mouse to come out.'

'Did it?'

'No, well, I didn't see it, so I suppose it's still there.'

'So you now have a shrew loose,' I said.

Hilda looked at me for a moment with raised eyebrows and then gave her little gruff bark of laughter. 'Precisely.'

I hadn't seen Janet Williams for some years,

but she's the sort of person who, when they've reached their forties, never seems to change. Her hair, once a soft russet brown was now just dull mouse and streaked with grey, but her face was almost unlined and her clear grey eyes looked out as sharply as ever from behind the same kind of light tortoiseshell spectacles she always used to wear.

'Well now,' she said, as we shook hands, 'this is something of a unique occasion.'

'I suppose it is.'

'Well, when we were at St Hilda's together all those years ago, I don't imagine either of us envisaged this particular situation. Poor Beth! It really is a tragedy. She should have had so many more years, so many more books to be written, she was at the height of her powers.'

'Yes, it's dreadfully sad.'

'I'm very touched,' Janet went on, 'that she left her papers to this library. It will be a most important collection.'

'You knew that she was going to do that?'

'Oh yes, she wrote to me some months ago saying that was what she wanted to do and I told her how grateful we would be – but, of course, I never expected that it would be so soon!'

We were both silent for a moment and then Janet said, 'What form do the papers take? And how many are there?'

I described the contents as best I could. 'I think they should be transferred here as soon as possible, in case people want to work on them.'

'Yes, there's no problem there. They'll have to go to Conservation, of course, but if you want to use them – or if there is any special reason why some bona fide scholar needs to look at them – then we will try to accommodate you.'

'There are some more, actually, down at the cottage,' I said. 'Mostly letters, I believe, and I imagine John will want to look through them first.'

'Well now,' Janet said briskly, 'I'll send the van to Kew to pick up what's there and then the rest can come as and when. Would next Monday morning suit you? Will you be there yourself?'

'Yes, that's fine. I'll arrange to be there. It will give me time to have photocopies made of the things I'll be working on.'

'Splendid. I'll get the Conservation people alerted. I expect to get quite a few enquiries as soon as people know where the papers are. You will have to give written permission, of course, before anyone can have access, and especially if they want to do any photocopying.'

'Goodness,' I sighed, 'it is complicated!'

'Well, Beth was a very important writer and it is only natural that there will be a great deal of interest in the background to her novels.'

'I really am beginning to wonder if I've taken on more than I can manage,' I said to Hilda that evening.

'Nonsense,' she said. 'Beth wouldn't have appointed you if she hadn't the fullest confidence in your capabilities.'

'It's all a bit daunting, just dealing with the papers, let alone writing the biography and preparing the short stories for press.'

'It will make a nice change for you. You spend far too much time down in Taviscombe.'

Hilda, London born and bred, can never imagine how anyone could contemplate living anywhere else. To her it is the unique and perfect centre of the universe. 'At the *heart* of things,' as she always says.

'I don't like leaving Michael for too long—' I protested.

'Do him good,' Hilda said firmly. 'You mollycoddle that boy, not that he is a boy any more. He's perfectly able to look after things and, anyway, he's probably delighted to have the place to himself.'

'You're probably right,' I said ruefully. 'I sometimes hear myself telling him to wear a scarf or put his gloves on, just as though he's six years old. Isn't that awful! He's very patient with me!'

'Michael is a splendid young man,' Hilda said, 'and I'm very fond of him, but it will be an excellent thing for you each to get on with your own lives for a while.'

Before I could reply, there was an interruption when a small white tornado burst into the room, leaped onto the arm of the sofa and began to sharpen his claws.

'Tolly darling!' Hilda protested mildly.

I picked the little cat up and held him up in front of me.

'Bad boy! You know you mustn't do that!'

He regarded me complacently, purring loudly, then he bit my wrist sharply and wriggled free.

'He wants his supper,' Hilda said lovingly. 'Don't you, my precious?'

Tolly gave a loud cry and walked from the room in the direction of the kitchen, his tail held high, while I pondered on the power of love, in whatever form it might manifest itself.

Chapter Five

I made photocopies of the manuscripts I wanted and Beth's papers were duly despatched to the Senate House Library. Reluctantly I sent a copy of the novel to Ralph and settled down to do some editorial work on the short stories. I found editing someone else's work rather than struggling with my own positively enjoyable and working in Hilda's study, which she had kindly made over to me, was, once Tolly had been rigorously excluded, really quite restful. Time passed very pleasantly – I almost felt that I was on holiday – and though I rang Michael occasionally to see that all was well, I took Hilda's words to heart and decided that it would be good for us both to occupy our own space for a while.

Hilda and I were sitting over a late breakfast one morning. Tolly having gone off first thing ('I'm really quite worried – he hasn't had any breakfast'), we were able to read the morning papers in peace. I was just looking despairingly at a page of the latest fashions (transparent tops, skirts shorter than ever, everything in shades of virulent lime and tangerine, all worn with what appeared to be gardening boots) when an exclamation from Hilda made me look up.

'Your friend John Blackmore seems to be in financial trouble,' she said.

'Really? what sort of trouble?'

'Just a minute, I'll read you what it says.' She picked up her *Financial Times*. 'Where is it? Oh, here we are. "United Nations sources today confirmed that UNRA funding of the Dahomey River Dam project has been withdrawn following the recent coup in the West African state of Ashanti. This latest blow to Blackmore International, the principal contractors, has revived City speculation that the privately

98

owned civil engineering group will have to ask its bankers for its debts to be re-structured. Chairman John Blackmore was not available for comment yesterday."'

'Oh dear,' I said. 'Poor John! As if he hadn't enough to cope with just now!'

'In view of all this, I imagine he's had a lot on his mind for some time.'

'I suppose so. I thought he was looking pretty awful when I saw him – I put it down to Beth's death, naturally, but if he's had financial worries hanging over him as well–'

'Where is he now?' Hilda asked.

'He was going to Düsseldorf, but I suppose he might be back by now. I wonder if I ought to ring him? I've still got the key to the house at Kew, which is a bit of a responsibility.'

'I should think he'll have most of the financial press breathing down his neck for the next few days,' Hilda said wryly. 'I'd leave it for a while, if I were you.'

'Yes, you're right.' I leaned forward and took another slice of toast. 'Goodness, I've just thought of something. He was talking about selling the cottage. I assumed it was because of Beth dying there, but perhaps he actually needed to.'

'I don't imagine what he would get for one cottage – even one in the Cotswolds – would go very far towards settling his financial difficulties.'

'No, I suppose not.'

'Mind you, I imagine Beth's estate will go to him and I gather from what you have told me that she was a very wealthy woman in her own right.'

'Yes, she made masses of money from those two films, but one never thought about it somehow because John was so rich.'

'He may be glad of it now.'

'Oh dear, yes, I expect he will. It's just that it's rather awful to think of it like that.'

Hilda raised her eyebrows. 'My dear Sheila, facts are facts, especially in the world of finance.'

'Anyway, if Beth was alive she'd have given him whatever she had.'

'I'm sure you are right.'

John telephoned me the following day. Naturally I didn't say anything to him about what I'd read about his business problems.

'I really must return your key,' I said. 'Shall I bring it round?'

'Actually,' he said, 'I've got all the stuff from the cottage that you might like to look over, so perhaps you'd better keep it for a bit. It would be nice to see you, though. Could you possibly come round tomorrow? I'd take you to lunch or something, but I rather need to be here for most of to-morrow–'

'No, really, that will be fine. And I'd like to take the opportunity to see the things from the cottage – I think you said it was mostly letters – so that I can check what needs to go to the library. Would ten o'clock be too early? Then perhaps I could spend a few hours on the papers.'

'That's great. Thank you, Sheila, for all you're doing. The children and I appreciate it very much.'

'How are they? Is Mark any better?'

'I still haven't seen him, though we've spoken a couple of times on the phone. I've had to be away quite a bit.' He paused. 'You may have heard,' he said, 'I have a few problems at the moment. My business–'

'Yes,' I said. 'I'm very sorry.'

'It's just that it's all going to take a lot of sorting out and I feel I'm letting Mark and Helen down badly, not being around for them just now.'

'I'm sure they understand,' I said. 'They're not children, they know how things are.'

When I arrived at Kew the next day a suitcase and an airline bag were in the hall.

John saw me looking at them and smiled wearily.

'I'm having to go back to Düsseldorf again tomorrow,' he said.

'You must be worn out,' I said.

'It's not the happiest of times,' he said.

I followed him into the kitchen, where he had some coffee ready. Half a dozen more cardboard boxes were piled up in a corner and he gestured towards them.

'That's the lot now. Mostly letters, as I said.'

'Have you been through them yourself? I mean, is there anything personal there that you won't want to go into the archive?'

'I'm afraid I've left that to you. They're mostly in files – labelled – and at a quick glance they all seem to be your sort of stuff. You know, prominent literary figures!' He gave a little laugh. 'Letters from them and Beth's letters to them.'

'She kept copies?'

'Yes, mostly, I think. To be honest, I never took as much interest as I suppose I should in that side of her life. Of course I knew how eminent she was, how famous, and then there was all that film stuff. But Beth understood that that wasn't my scene. We had other things–'

I smiled at him affectionately. 'I know,' I said.

'If there is anything you think I ought to

see, just put it to one side and I'll try and get around to looking at it when I can.'

I pushed my coffee cup to one side. 'Actually, there *is* something I'd like your opinion about.'

'Oh?'

'There's a novel,' I said. 'It's quite complete, but it isn't at all in her usual style. I found it very disturbing.'

'How do you mean?'

'It's hard to explain – it's all a bit, well, over the top, I suppose. To be honest, I found it hard to imagine Beth writing it.'

'All a bit steamy, do you mean?' He looked at me enquiringly.

'No.' I shook my head. 'Nothing like that. Just a sort of raw energy and passion – very odd. The thing is, I stupidly told Ralph Hastings about it and he was very keen to publish it. I should think it might well be a bit of a literary sensation. But I honestly don't think Beth would have wanted it to be published. I got the impression that she wrote it just for herself.'

'To see if she could, you mean? Trying out something different that didn't come off?'

'Yes,' I said, 'something like that, perhaps. I told Ralph what I think, but you know how persistent he can be. So I'd like you to read it and, if you agreed with me, then Ralph would have to let it drop. After all, you hold the copyright.'

'Yes, well, I'll certainly do that. But I'm afraid it won't be for a while. As you can imagine I'm up to my eyes in things just now.'

'Of course. Any time will do.' I was silent for a moment and then I said tentatively, 'John, I'm so very sorry about all this – the business and so forth. It must be a dreadful time for you, coming just now.'

'It doesn't help. Actually, people are very good and I think I should be able to turn things round eventually, but it's going to be damned hard. One thing, though,' he said, 'Helen's been absolutely wonderful. Not just sympathetic and understanding, but in practical ways as well.'

'Really?'

'Yes, well,' he hesitated and then spoke quickly, 'Beth left her estate equally between me and the children. There's a great deal of money involved. Now Helen has insisted on making over her share to help me through this particular difficulty. Of course I couldn't let her just *give* me the money. It will be an extended loan and I'll repay it as soon as things are straightened out. But I was very touched, as you can imagine.'

'That was very generous of her,' I said.

'Actually,' John went on, 'I feel particularly bad about having to go away tomorrow. I've got all the documents for her to sign and I was going to Cambridge to see her myself and thank her again. But they really should be signed as quickly as possible, so I suppose I'll have to let the lawyers do the whole thing–' He looked at me for a moment and then said suddenly, 'Sheila, could I ask you a really big favour? Could *you* go and give her the documents and have a little chat with her – let her know how much it's all meant to me?'

I looked at him in surprise.

'No,' he said, 'it's too much to ask. It wouldn't be fair.'

'Nonsense! Of course I'll go. I can easily go there and back in a day. It will be a nice little outing for me.'

'Really?'

'Absolutely. I haven't seen Helen for several years, but we always got on very well. I'd love to see her again.'

I took an early train to Cambridge and didn't take a taxi from the station, but walked along Regent Street, looking at all the changes that had been made since I was there last. It was a lovely day and I walked slowly up Petty Cury, through Market Square and into King's Parade, standing for a while to admire the delicate tracery towers of the college and chapel.

John had telephoned Helen, who said she had a lecture in the morning but would be back in college by midday. To fill in the time I went into the Copper Kettle for a coffee and amused myself by listening to the undergraduates who had surged in after their eleven o'clock lecture. From their conversation I realized that it was not only the buildings that had changed. These young people were much more conscious of the world outside than we had been in my far-off student days. We had been so very concerned with our own lives, inward-looking, content to enjoy being under-graduates, being young and alive after a long period of postwar austerity. Just a few, people like Bill North, looked to other, more serious things, but they were the ex-ception. I know the world has changed so much since then and it's no longer possible to live in that particular ivory tower. Still, I felt sorry for this new generation, who have never known the kind of innocent delight in things that we felt all those years ago. The world, as I now see it, with the dew still upon it, and a hope, perhaps naïve, but a real hope nevertheless, that life was going to be fresh and exciting. The undergraduates drifted away to their next lecture, and I too got up and went out into the sunshine.

As I wandered along the corridors of Newnham looking for Helen's room, I turned over in my mind how I should approach the subject of Beth's death. There had obviously been some sort of tension between them, though Beth apparently hadn't known why. I wondered if I should tackle it head-on, or simply avoid the subject and concentrate solely on what John had asked of me. When I knocked on the white-painted door I still hadn't decided. I would have to wait and see how things developed.

Helen was now a young woman and no longer the schoolgirl I had known. With her long chestnut hair and large grey eyes set under rather heavy brows, she was enough like Beth at the same age to make me catch my breath for a moment. She greeted me kindly but, I thought, warily.

'Thank you for coming,' she said. 'It was very good of you. I know Daddy's very grateful.'

I gave her the documents. 'I'm sure you know how much what you have done means to him,' I said. 'It was a very generous thing to do.'

She shook her head. 'No, it wasn't. I had no intention of taking Mother's money.'

'But why?'

'Personal reasons,' she said.

There was a moment's silence. Then I tried again.

'Poor John – it's terrible, all this coming just now, so soon after your mother's death, especially since he seems to blame himself for that.'

'That's ridiculous!'

'I know, but he thinks that if he had been there he might have prevented that dreadful accident.'

'She chose to go down to the cottage alone – that is, if she *was* alone–' She broke off as if she had said too much.

'What do you mean?' I asked. 'What is all this?'

She looked at me resentfully. 'What's the

use of talking to you? You were *her* friend, you're on her side, not Daddy's.'

'It's not a question of taking sides,' I said. 'Look, you're obviously very upset about something. Have you told your father?'

'No. No, I can't. He's the last person I can tell, it would make him so unhappy.'

'Then do you think you could tell me?'

'You?'

'It's true that I was your mother's oldest friend, but I've known your father for a very long time – before you were born. I'm very fond of him and I'm sure that if he knew you were troubled he'd want me to try and do something about it. Now don't you think that's true?'

'I suppose so,' she replied slowly.

'Bottling things up isn't good, you know.'

'No, you're right, I have to tell somebody.' She moved over towards the door. 'It's stifling in here, let's go outside.'

We walked across the garden in silence and sat on a bench under a large copper beech.

'Now then,' I said. 'Tell me what's wrong.'

Helen clasped her hands together as if for support and sat without speaking for a few minutes. Finally, 'It's my mother,' she said. 'She was having an affair.'

'Are you sure?' I asked, unable to take in the fact she had stated so baldly.

'Oh yes, I'm sure.'

'How did you find out?'

'My friend Julia saw her when she was on holiday in the Greek islands. On Hydra, it was.'

'And she was sure it was your mother?'

'Yes. Julia knew her quite well – she used to stay with us for holidays.'

'What exactly happened?'

Helen picked up a leaf and began to pick it to pieces. 'Julia was on one of those island trips – you know, the boat calls at a number of places, Aegina, Poros, Hydra. Anyway, Julia and her sister were having coffee in an outdoor café by the harbour when she saw my mother sitting at another table a little way away. There was a man with her, but he had his back to Julia so she couldn't see his face. She was just going to go over and say hello to Mother when they both got up and walked away.'

'But, Helen, that doesn't prove anything. Beth was doing research in Greece – it could very well have been someone who was helping her–'

'Not really.' Helen's voice was hard. 'They walked away with their arms around each other and, as they walked, the man bent and kissed her.'

'Oh, Helen.'

'You see how I could never tell my father? He adored her, it would break his heart, even now–' Her eyes were full of tears and she brushed them away impatiently. 'How could she *do* that to him,' she burst out. 'How could she cheat and lie when he trusted her?'

She turned to me. 'Did you know about it?' she demanded fiercely. 'Did she boast to you about her new conquest? How many others were there?'

'Helen, don't! Please. You'll make yourself ill! Honestly, I had absolutely no idea. I always thought Beth and your father had a perfect marriage.'

She laughed bitterly. 'We all thought so. And all the time she was living a lie.'

'How long ago was this?'

'About a year.'

'And that's why you were never at home?'

'How could I bear to see her with my father when I *knew*–'

'No, I can see that. She told me – she said she was worried about you.'

'And all the time she was carrying on with God knows who. The hypocrisy! It makes me sick! I hate her, I still hate her and I always will!' I couldn't think what to say, so I simply laid my hand on hers. This seemed to calm her a little and she said more quietly, 'Poor Daddy. He must never know, I couldn't bear it if he did.'

I knew that Helen had always been very close to her father, as Mark had been to Beth, but I hadn't realized quite how deeply the division in the family had gone. I wondered now if perhaps Helen had resented her mother, had wanted her father's undivided attention and this evidence of what she saw as Beth's betrayal had pushed her over from unconscious resentment into actual hatred.

'No, you are quite right,' I said, 'he mustn't know.' She gave me a grateful look and I asked tentatively, 'What about Mark? Did you tell him?'

'No, he'd gone off with that Fiona woman and, anyway,' she gave a scornful laugh, 'he'd never believe anything against Mother, he was always her favourite.'

I thought it better not to reply to this. Helen was not in the mood to listen to anything she didn't want to hear.

'So you see,' she said, 'why I couldn't take her money or her jewellery, all the things Daddy gave her. You do see?'

'Yes,' I said. 'And now you will be able to help your father. He needs that money just now.'

'It's awful being stuck here in Cambridge when I could be at home looking after him. I offered to leave, but he wouldn't let me.'

'I'm sure he wants you to stay on here and do well in your Tripos. You're reading history, aren't you? He's very proud of you.'

She nodded. 'Thank you for listening. You're right, it has helped a bit.'

'Good. Now, let's go and find something to eat. I had particular instructions from John to give you a really good lunch – I think he believes they starve you here!'

'No, the food's pretty fair.' She got up. 'I'll just go to my room to get a coat and then we'll go. There's a good place in Trinity Street.'

As we walked back towards the college, I admired the garden, especially the drifts of tall irises in delicate colours, bronze and pale lemon and mauve and pink.

'Yes,' Helen said, 'it is lovely, isn't it? There's a story that, when it was first founded, the college was offered money to build a chapel, but they chose to spend the

116

money on a garden instead. I don't know if it's true, but I like to think so.'

As we walked through Newnham village and then across the Fen to Mill Lane, we talked of general things, the college and her work, the social life at Cambridge, anything to avoid the topic that was uppermost in our minds.

After lunch, as we said goodbye, I said, 'Try and put all this behind you. It's all over now, don't let it ruin *your* life. You're young, you have so much in front of you. I know that's what John would want.'

'It was good of you to listen.'

'I'm always there,' I said, 'if ever you want to talk. John has my address, in London and in Taviscombe. Just pick up the phone.'

'I will. Thank you for everything. Tell Daddy I'll get the documents back to Mr Musgrove tomorrow.' She looked at her watch. 'I'd better dash. I've got a supervision at four o'clock and I've got to fetch my essay.'

'What's it on?'

'The effect of English foreign policy under Melbourne.'

'Oh, a splendid man, almost too good looking. No wonder the young Victoria fell for him!'

She gave me a polite smile and I reflected that Helen, like the undergraduates in the Copper Kettle, had something of the Matthew Arnold strain of 'high seriousness' that we, more frivolous, graduates of Oxford always associated with Cambridge.

As I watched her walk away down Silver Street I felt that I had, in some small way, been of help. I'd done what John (and Beth) would have wanted, I'd tried to comfort their daughter.

Chapter Six

It took me some time to come to terms with the idea of Beth having had an affair. I discussed it with Hilda (I knew she was the soul of discretion) one evening.

'I still can't believe it,' I said. 'I thought she and John were so happy together. Of course, they led their own lives to a certain extent, but, when they were together, it always seemed to me there was great affection there.'

'There probably still was,' Hilda said. 'I expect Beth went on being fond of John right to the end.'

'I suppose so.'

'But when people are in love – or think they are in love – they conveniently forget everything and everyone else. Or so,' she added dispassionately, 'I am led to believe, since that particular experience has never come my way.'

I looked at her curiously. 'Have you never been in love?' I asked.

It was something I had always wondered about, but Hilda was not a person you could put that sort of question to, except, perhaps, in this context, since she'd brought the matter up herself.

'No,' she said, 'I have never found a man – or a woman, for that matter – for whom it would be worth giving up any part of my own life and thoughts. I have always believed in the superiority of reason over emotion and the intrusion of anything so irrational was quite unacceptable to me. Naturally, I realize that I have probably been the loser by all this, but that is some-thing I have managed to accept with equanimity.'

I glanced across at the bureau, where there was a photograph of Hilda as a young woman, which she kept only (since she greatly disliked photographs of herself and always walked away if one produced a camera) because it was a group which included her parents. She had been a very attractive girl, small and neat, with dark curly hair and large expressive eyes, though with more than a hint of the sternness that now characterized her appearance.

'But I'm sure,' I said, taking the opportunity of probing a little since she seemed in an unusually mellow mood, 'someone – several people – must have been in love with you.'

She smiled slightly, as if in reminiscence. 'There was someone, during the war.'

'Who was it? What happened?'

'His name was Hugh Johnson. He worked at Bletchley Park for a while.'

'And?'

'I told him I had no feelings for him.' She looked at me sharply. 'Besides, the atmosphere in that place was, not surprisingly given the circumstances of our being there, most claustrophobic. People's emotions were magnified; it was an unnatural situation.'

'Poor man,' I said sadly. 'What happened to him?'

'He left Bletchley Park soon after. I heard later that he had been parachuted into France to help the Resistance. I don't think he returned.'

I looked at Hilda. She seemed unmoved by these revelations, but I noticed that she turned her head away, as if to avoid any scrutiny on my part.

The door burst open and a small, white, furry body hurled himself across the room, jumped up on to the back of Hilda's armchair and began to bat at her hair with his paw. She reached up and put him on her lap, stroking the small, triangular head, a slight satisfied smile playing about her lips.

'Well,' she said, 'it's almost Tolly's bedtime. Would you like a hot drink, Sheila?'

'That would be nice,' I said, getting up. 'I'll go and make some hot chocolate for us both, shall I?'

The following morning I had a letter from

an American scholar. A Dr Phoebe Walters wanted to meet me to discuss a proposed critical biography of Dame Elizabeth Blackmore, which was to be financed by a grant from the Templar Foundation, of which I had doubtless heard. She was, herself, the author of a life of Alice Duer Millar and various papers on women's studies. She would be in England for a year and would be grateful for an early meeting since she was anxious to begin work on the Blackmore papers, which she understood were now lodged in the Senate House Library. She remained mine sincerely.

'Oh dear,' I said to Hilda. 'It's started.'

'What's started?'

'The bandwagoning.'

'What?'

'That's what Philip Larkin called it. Whenever a well-known author dies, American scholars immediately leap on to the bandwagon with biographies, studies, bibliographies – the lot.'

'Well,' she replied reasonably, 'you did

expect it, and you did know what was involved in being a literary executor.'

'Yes, I know I did, it's just that it all seems so *soon*. I suppose I'd better write to the woman. She sounds frighteningly efficient.'

'Your term – semester, is that what they call it? – at that American college should have prepared you to face the most formidable American academic.'

'Oh dear, I haven't been through those letters yet – the ones John passed on to me, the ones from the cottage. I think perhaps I'd better get them to the library so that they can be accessioned and try and look through them there. Besides,' I added, 'there, they're less likely to be pounced on and chewed by Tolly. He really is a demon for paper.'

'I know! And he's taken to biting the corners of books,' Hilda said. 'I can't read in bed any more.'

When I went to the library, Janet took me up to one of the top floors in the tower, where the collection was housed. Since the ascent was in a tiny, ancient lift that jerked from side to side in its progress upwards, I was glad when we reached our destination in safety and I could stop holding my breath.

'Sorry about the lift,' Janet said, 'a fearful squash for more than one person and *very* rickety! But it's that or climbing up thirteen flights of stairs. Right then, here we are and here's Rachel Edwards, who will be looking after the collection. Rachel, this is Sheila Malory, Elizabeth Blackmore's literary executor. She will have to give permission for people to examine the papers or photocopy them – but you know all that. I'll leave you then, Sheila, in Rachel's capable hands.'

She stepped back into the lift, closed the doors and disappeared from view.

Rachel Edwards was a small, slight girl with soft brown hair and a worried expression.

'The papers have been accessioned, but

I'm afraid Conservation haven't dealt with the latest ones. We're very short-staffed at the moment. It's the cuts.'

Her voice was low and difficult to hear, as mouselike as her appearance, and I thought of her as a little Beatrix Potter figure, tucked away up here in her own little world, away from the everyday bustle downstairs.

'Never mind,' I said reassuringly, 'I only want to have a quick look through the letters today, just to make sure there's nothing personal still in there.'

'Oh dear.' She looked even more worried. 'They've been accessioned – I don't think it would be possible to *remove* anything–'

'I don't expect there is anything. But if there is, we'll simply put a restriction on it. Would that be all right?'

Her face cleared. 'Yes, that would be perfectly in order. The papers are stored in here.' She gestured towards a sort of enormous wire cage, inside which were rows of shelves on which reposed file-boxes, presumably holding documents.

'I always think those cage things in stack rooms are funny,' I said. 'As if the documents were wild animals that needed to be restrained!'

She looked at me blankly, then, realizing that I was attempting a joke, gave me a polite smile. 'If you would like to sit down at one of the desks by the window,' she said, 'I'll bring you the letters a box at a time.'

I went meekly over to the row of desks and sat down.

The letters were, as John had said, to and from the great and good in the literary world. I didn't read them all through carefully, merely glancing at each one to make a quick note of its contents. There were quite a few from Ralph Hastings, mostly couched in affectionate, almost ingratiating, terms, and several letters from Emma Foxwell, trying to get Beth to publish with Coda Press. I looked with some curiosity at Beth's replies to these. It seemed to me that she had been tempted by the very generous terms (including a major publicity campaign of the sort that Ralph could never have afforded) that had been outlined. I wondered whether, if she had lived, she might, however reluctantly, have left Ralph.

I put these particular letters to one side, feeling that it would be unsuitable for the wider public to see them, and went on with my task. It was with some surprise that I came upon letters to and from myself. I had settled into an academic mode, looking at the letters before me simply as 'material' to be used in research, and the sight of my correspondence – some of it in my own handwriting – brought home to me the salutary fact that all 'material' is actually part of a real person's life and should be treated accordingly.

After a few hours I had a small pile of letters I thought should be withheld from researchers and I handed them over to Rachel Edwards.

'The rest are OK,' I said. 'There's no problem there. But if you can put a restriction on these–'

'Very well, Mrs Malory. I'll see to that.'

'Next week', I said, 'I hope to come in and start going through some of the manuscripts I haven't had time to deal with yet. Will that be possible?'

'I think most of the manuscripts should be back from Conservation by then,' she said. 'Then there'll just be the letters to do.'

'Good, that's fine. Oh, by the way, a Dr Phoebe Walters may be coming in to look at the papers. I'll be seeing her in a few days' time and I'll let you know when she wants to come. She's writing a critical biography of Dame Elizabeth.'

'Yes, I see. If you could just give her *written* permission–'

'Of course. Right then, I'll see you next week.'

She gave another mouse-like murmur that I took to be assent and I went away.

Not wishing to entrust myself to the ancient lift, I walked all the way down the thirteen flights of stairs and, by the time I got to the bottom, I was pretty exhausted, so I made my way round the back of the British Museum to a pub I sometimes used to go to with Beth. It was still early, so the place wasn't very full. I got a gin and tonic from the bar and went over and sat in a corner at the far end. I took a book from my shopping bag and was just settling down for a quiet read when I was aware of someone standing by my table. I looked up and saw, to my surprise, that it was Ralph Hastings.

'Good gracious,' I exclaimed. 'Fancy seeing you here!' He raised his eyebrows. 'I work not far away,' he said. 'This is my local.'

'Yes, of course.'

'May I join you?'

'Oh yes, please do.'

He put his glass on the table and sat down opposite me.

'I've just been in the Senate House Library,' I said. 'Going through Beth's letters.'

'Her letters?' He looked startled.

'Yes, you know, in the archive, with the manuscripts.'

'Ah, yes, I see.'

'There were some of yours,' I said chattily, 'and some of mine too. It felt odd, finding them there.'

'Yes, I suppose it did.'

I could see that he was wondering which of his letters Beth had kept and what I had made of them. Then, apparently recovering himself, he said, 'Do you think there might be a volume there? Collections of letters are very popular now and I imagine Beth's correspondence was quite wide and of some interest.'

'I don't know,' I said doubtfully. 'I don't think there'd be enough.'

'Well, in any case,' he continued smoothly, 'you will be able to use the best of them in the biography, won't you?'

'Yes, I suppose so.'

There was a pause while we both sipped our drinks and then Ralph said, 'I'm glad to have this opportunity for a talk with you.

131

of Beth's novel and, frankly, I must tell you that I am very excited about it.'

'Are you?' I said cautiously.

'Very excited indeed.' He leaned forward. 'It is, as you observed, in an entirely different style from her other work and therefore *immensely* important.'

'Important?'

'Naturally,' he said impatiently. 'Not only for the general reader but to scholars writing on her work. It is an amazing find!'

'But it's so raw,' I said, 'the style is so... I don't know how to describe it. So rough and unpolished.'

'Exactly! New and vibrant!'

'I honestly don't think she meant it for publication,' I said obstinately. 'I mean, it looks to me as if she wrote it a little while ago. If, as you say, she was starting on something new, something she *wanted* published, surely she'd have shown it to you before now.'

'No, no,' he said. 'Beth often put things to

one side – to mature, as it were, before she actually submitted them. That was the way she worked.'

'Well,' I began doubtfully, 'that may be so–'

'I'm sure that's what happened,' Ralph broke in, 'especially with something quite new like this.'

'But it's so personal,' I said.

'All writing is personal.'

'Yes, in a way. But most writers feel the need to *refine* their experiences, to sift the wheat from the chaff, as it were, before actually using them in their work. That's what Beth did in her other books.'

'But, don't you see,' Ralph said urgently, 'that's what makes this so exciting. This is a writer giving us a report from the battle zone! What you think of as roughness of style and technique is actually power, that is what makes it so compelling.'

'That may be so,' I said, 'but I still can't believe that Beth, who was such a reserved person, would want all this raw emotion made public.'

'You think, then,' Ralph said, raising his eyebrows slightly, 'that this is all personal, something she actually experienced herself? Is that what you're trying to say?'

I felt flustered. 'Yes, perhaps – I don't know – that's something we can't possibly– All I know is that I wouldn't feel happy about having it published.'

'Who is this man?' Ralph said. 'Not John, presumably. Was she having an affair?'

'No, of course not.' I felt my face flushing. I'm not very good at lying. 'I never suggested that she was.'

'But you think that somehow this book is related to her personal life?'

'Yes – no. Not exactly *that*–'

Ralph smiled his superior smile. 'My dear Sheila, we must try to think logically about this. Either the book is some sort of reflection of her personal life and, therefore, in your view unsuitable for publication, or else it is pure fiction and to be judged simply on its literary merits. Now I think that as a piece of literature it is very exciting

– important, even, as I have explained.'

'I didn't care for it,' I said. 'As a piece of literature. It's not the sort of book I like – nor, I believe will any of her regular readers. I think it will do her reputation considerable harm.'

'And I,' Ralph said, with his most charming smile, 'believe it will bring many *new* readers, who may then turn to the main body of her work. Think of Forster's *Maurice*.'

'That was quite different,' I said irritably. 'That was a finished piece of work, properly crafted – this is not.'

Ralph shifted his ground. 'Has John read it yet?'

'No. Poor John – with all his financial worries, he's hardly had time to do any reading! I certainly wouldn't dream of bothering him with it at the moment!'

'Oh, yes.' Ralph looked thoughtful. 'Of course. I had heard something. Is it serious, do you think?'

'Yes, very serious. But I think he's

gradually getting on top of it. But it will take time and he will be abroad a lot. And, of course, we can do nothing until John has read it. So you see,' I concluded triumphantly, 'we'll just have to leave it for now.'

'Yes. Yes, indeed.' Ralph smiled again. 'Now then, let me get you another drink. What is it? Gin and tonic?'

'No, really,' I said, 'it's very kind of you, but I have to go now.' I reached for my shopping bag under the table. 'I'll see that John reads the manuscript as soon as I can.'

I somehow felt the need to get as far away as possible from Ralph, so I jumped on a bus and got off at Bond Street where I took refuge in the basement café of Fenwick's and there, among the young PAs and Girl Fridays eating their prawn salads and drinking their mineral water, I considered Beth's novel.

Was it based on real people? The way it was written seemed to suggest it. And the heroine, too. Beth had always ignored the good points of her appearance, her beautiful chestnut hair and her tall slim figure, but, as girls do, agonized over what she considered her defects – her nose, she felt, was too large, her mouth too wide, her feet too big, her height a disadvantage. In effect she always thought of herself as plain, not realizing that anyone with her warmth and vitality could never be considered so. The heroine of the book, then, was obviously Beth. But who was the main figure, the rich industrialist, the man of power? It certainly wasn't John. This man was driven by ambition in a way John never had been, he was ruthless and in some ways cruel, as John, kind, gentle John, could never be. Above all, he had the kind of charisma that I certainly had never actually encountered in real life. Only the eye of love could see such things in another human being.

Which brought me back to the problem of Beth's lover. Was this the man? If so, who on earth could it be? I worried away at the problem for a while, but it seemed insoluble.

I got up, went over to the counter and got

myself a large slab of cheesecake. I felt I needed this sweet and cloying comfort to make up for what, I felt, had been a really difficult and trying morning.

Chapter Seven

I had arranged to meet Phoebe Walters at my club. Since she sounded rather formidable and since I was new to the whole business of being a literary executor, I thought that the more formal surroundings might give me a slightly greater air of authority. In the event, she didn't seem formidable at all. She was younger than I expected – in her late twenties – and rather pretty, with dark-brown curly hair and an attractive smile.

'It's so good of you to see me like this, Mrs Malory,' she said. 'I'm sure you must be busy and a pushy American is probably the very last thing you need right now!'

'No,' I said, 'not at all. I mean, I certainly didn't think of you as a pushy American. Will you have coffee?'

'Yes, please. Decaff, if they have it.'

We talked for a while about Beth and her work. At least, Phoebe talked and I listened. I must confess that my heart always sinks when I hear the phrase 'sub-text', but certainly her approach to the novels did seem to me to be sensible and perceptive.

'Naturally, I would like to draw parallels between her life and her work,' Phoebe said. 'And it would be really valuable if I could have access to the papers as soon as possible. I do have a kind of deadline, and though it isn't absolutely rigid, I need to get started as soon as possible. I have a year's sabbatical from my teaching post and I plan to spend six or nine months in England doing the research.'

'Yes, of course,' I replied. 'Actually, I have spoken to the librarian at the Senate House and she will be expecting you. I must just write a formal letter for you to take along. I think I have your London address on the letter you wrote to me.'

'I'm sharing a house in west London with

two other girls.'

'Oh, really? Whereabouts?'

'Just off Ealing Common. Do you know it?'

'Yes. I'm staying with my cousin, who lives not far away in Holland Park. So we are both on the District Line. Will you have a biscuit?'

'I shouldn't really – I'll be fat as a pig! But one of the things I love most about England is the chocolate digestives!' She took a biscuit and continued, 'I guess I ought to know exactly what material I can use. I mean, if you are writing the official bio-graphy–'

'I must confess I haven't been through all the papers yet, so I don't know *what* I'll be using. I think the best thing will be for you to tell me what particular things you want to quote and we'll see if we can come to some arrangement.'

Phoebe looked at me curiously. 'You're being very generous,' she said. 'Forgive me asking, but do you realize quite what a literary gold mine you're sitting on?'

'Gold mine?'

'Yes. A whole new author, virtually untouched, and one of the foremost literary figures of our day! You won't believe how much material there will be in the Blackmore papers for doctoral theses and critical studies, not to mention all the works offered for security of tenure in colleges all over the States!'

I laughed. 'You absolutely horrify me! Will it really be as bad as that?'

Phoebe smiled back. 'Worse, probably! I can't believe I'm first in the field.' She absently took another biscuit. 'Seriously, though, I'll be concentrating on the lit crit side of things, but there'll be a whole raft of people who'll want to write about Elizabeth Blackmore's life, so I do think you must be careful about allowing access to people who'll be trying to get in first with a biographical study, before your own Life is published. You don't want that!'

'No, I suppose I don't. Oh dear,' I sighed,

'there's so much to think about.'

'It's dog eat dog out there,' Phoebe said cheerfully. 'Actually,' she continued, 'I'd be really grateful if you could spare me an hour sometime, when I've been through the papers, to answer a few questions. I mean, you were her oldest friend, you must know so much about her. Did she discuss her work with you?'

'No, not in recent years, anyway.'

'Still, you must have the key to a lot of the novels – how much she took from real life, people she knew. Stuff like that.'

'I'll do my best,' I said, 'but I'm not sure that I can be of much help.'

'Have you started to plan the biography yet?' Phoebe asked. 'It's excellent that you're the one to do it. The nineteenth-century novel isn't my field, but I've read all your books and papers and I admire them very much. I'm sure you'll do a great job.'

'That's very kind of you. I'm afraid I haven't read anything of yours–'

'Nothing's been published over here, there

isn't such an extensive market in Britain for women's studies. So far, anyway. But I have a couple of papers I could send you, if you're interested.'

'That would be kind of you.'

'She seemed very nice,' I said to Hilda that evening, over supper. 'Quite cosy, really, not too earnest and academic. Most intelligent.' I paused, wondering whether my view of her intelligence might possibly be coloured by her expressed admiration for my own work. 'Anyway, I'm sure she'll do a reasonable job. She didn't seem as jargon-ridden as some of them. Though I suppose I'll have to wait until I see the papers she's sending me before I can really judge. Some tremendously witty Americans I've met, who you'd think would write like angels, once they set pen to paper turn out the most turgid stuff!'

'I suppose they have to conform to the academic norm,' Hilda said. 'It's getting to be the same over here. No one takes you seriously as a scholar unless your prose is absolutely impenetrable. It takes a very brave spirit to swim against *that* particular tide.'

'I'm afraid you're right. How sad. Oh well, we'll just have to wait and see.'

I cut off a piece of cheese and was just about to put it on to my plate when a long, beige paw stretched up and neatly snatched it away.

'Oh, Tolly!'

'Oh dear,' Hilda said, 'I thought I'd shut him in the kitchen.' She got up and reached under the table. 'Come along, Tolly darling, just until we've had our food. You come and see what I've got for you outside—'

She came back into the room, shutting the door firmly behind her, and resumed her supper.

'I rather dread writing this biography,' I said. 'I mean, Beth was such a major figure, I'm afraid I won't do her justice.'

'Modesty is all very well,' Hilda said severely, 'but that sort of self-deprecation is just silly. Of course you can do it. You are a perfectly capable and experienced biographer.'

'Well, perhaps– But what's really worrying me is the fact that I won't be able to be honest.'

'What on earth do you mean?'

'This business about her having an affair. You see, it looks very much as if that unpublished novel has something to do with it and so – well – if it's part of her *writing*, then how can I avoid mentioning it? But I *can't* because of John. And not just John, other people might be hurt. Mark, for one. I don't suppose he knows about it. Besides, that part of her life was something she kept secret. How can I betray her like that? Oh, it's such a *muddle!*'

'I must say,' Hilda said, 'I have always deplored the way people tend to rush into print.'

'You think it's too soon?'

'If you want my honest opinion, yes, I do.'

'Ralph was very keen that I should do it as soon as possible,' I said.

'He would be. It's to his advantage. Especially if he's bringing out a new uniform edition of Beth's novels. An official biography would round that off nicely. A good commercial proposition.'

'Yes, that's true.'

'And didn't you say that it was possible Beth might have gone to another publisher?'

'It certainly looked like that from some of the letters I saw.'

'Well, in that case, all I can say is that her death has been very timely for him.'

'Hilda!'

'Actually,' Hilda went on, 'he isn't the only one, is he?'

'What on earth do you mean?'

'Well, John is going to be very grateful for her money just now, isn't he?'

'Really, Hilda! John *adored* Beth, and anyway, she would have given him the money if she'd been alive.'

'He couldn't be sure of that, though, could he? Especially if he knew about the lover. She might have been going to leave him.

And then there's Helen, who hated her mother and is going around saying that she's glad Beth is dead.'

'What on earth are you saying?' I asked.

'Nothing. Just that her death has been providential for some people.'

'You're not suggesting...? But that's ridiculous. Beth's death was a dreadful accident.'

'I'm not saying it wasn't, just that the facts need thinking about.'

I thought about Beth's son Mark the following day when I was in Notting Hill looking for a very special delicatessen that had been featured in the *Sunday Telegraph*, which had a certain kind of cheese that Hilda had expressed a wish to try. It was a pleasant day, so I was having what Rosemary and I call A Little Wander when I found myself in Pembridge Crescent. John had given me Mark's address, because I wanted to write to him after Beth died, and so on an impulse I turned into Pembridge

Gardens and looked for Number 2. It was a handsome Regency house with dazzling white stucco, two dark-blue front doors (the house was presumably divided into flats) with brass fittings, approached by a short flight of steps, decorated with planters full of immaculate flowers, and with all things handsome about it. I was just about to ring the bell of the ground-floor flat, marked Packard, and speak into the little microphone thing (something I always hate doing), when the door opened and a young man appeared. He was about nineteen and was wearing jeans, a T-shirt emblazoned with the faces of what I took to be some pop group (I have thankfully stopped trying to keep up with them since Michael reached the years of discretion) and the ubiquitous trainers.

'Oh, hello,' I said. 'Is Mark Blackmore at home?'

The young man called over his shoulder into the hall beyond, 'Mark! It's for you!' He turned to me and said 'Go on in.' Then he ran lightly down the steps and disappeared from view.

I stepped into the hall, which was dark after the bright sunlight outside. It was dark anyway, because it was decorated in rich reds and purples with a dark-blue carpet that exactly matched the colour of the front door. Very designer, I thought, very Fiona Packard. A voice called me from the end of the passage.

'Who is it? What do you want?'

I went towards it and found myself in a large room, very light and airy with blond wood furniture, cream curtains, covers and carpet and a great many enormous modern glass vases filled with expensive-looking flowers – the sort that you have to touch to see if they're real or artificial.

Mark was slumped on a vast chesterfield, which was covered in a cream, tweedy material. He was in distinct contrast to the elegant chic of the room. He was wearing crumpled pyjamas and a grubby towelling robe that had once been white. He was unshaven and his hair was greasy and unkempt.

'Who is it?' he asked irritably.

'Hello, Mark,' I said. 'It's Sheila Malory. I came to see how you are.'

He looked at me suspiciously. 'What do you mean, how I am?'

As he turned his head towards the light I was shocked at his appearance. His face was white and pasty and his eyes seemed sunk in, yet brilliant, almost as if he had a fever.

'I just wanted to see you,' I said, in what I hoped was a soothing manner. 'To say how very sorry I am about your mother. She was a very old and very dear friend. It was a terrible shock to us all. It must have been dreadful for you.'

'Yes,' he said in a dead voice. 'Dreadful.'

I began to wish I hadn't come. Mark's attitude, as well as his appearance, were disconcerting and upsetting. He had always seemed to me to be a charming boy, warm and affectionate. He had undeniable talent and had been very well thought of, so Beth

told me, in the demanding world of television. I couldn't imagine what had
happened to bring him down like this. I
knew he'd been devoted to Beth, but I
didn't think it was simply the fact of her
tragic death. From what she had told me
that last time we met, this change had
already begun then.

The silence grew between us, Mark not
attempting any kind of conversation. I tried
again. 'I expect you know that I'm your
mother's literary executor. Her publisher
wants me to write her life. Your father has no
objections, and I wondered what you
thought about it?'

He raised his head and stared at me, as if
he'd forgotten that anyone else was in the
room.

'Her life?' he repeated. 'What life?'

'Her biography,' I said, 'relating her life to
her work – that sort of thing.'

'What good will that do?'

'Well, I suppose it might help scholars and
people who are interested in her books.'

He gave a short, bitter laugh. 'Carrion crows picking over the corpse.'

'Oh no,' I protested, 'that's not fair. Your mother was a significant literary figure. What she wrote is in the public domain and the people who read her books, people who admire and respect them, will want to know more about her as a person—'

'It's nothing to do with them, nothing, do you hear me?'

He got up from the chesterfield and moved towards me, lurching as if he was drunk. I backed away and was wondering if he might even be going to attack me in some way when a woman's voice behind me said sharply, 'Who are you? How did you get in here?'

I turned and saw Fiona Packard standing in the doorway. I had met her once before at some book launch, when I had been fascinated and slightly repelled by her smart power-dressing, her poise and her self-assurance. Today, though, instead of the tailored suit and high heels, she was wearing white trousers and what was unmistakably a designer tunic in a bold navy and white pattern. She still looked quite formidable, indeed very angry, and I found myself explaining my presence rather incoherently.

'I'm Sheila Malory. Beth was a very dear friend. I came to see how Mark was. A young man let me in – he was just going out as I arrived–'

She made an exclamation of annoyance. 'That wretched boy – I told him to wait until I got back–' Then, pulling herself together with an effort, she said more calmly, 'I'm sorry. But Mark hasn't been well. He isn't allowed any visitors at present.' She turned towards him and said abruptly, 'Mark – go to your room.'

Mark, who had flung himself down in one of the armchairs, ignored her and appeared to show no interest in what was going on.

I found myself edging towards the door, apologizing as I went.

'Yes, of course, I quite understand. I'm sorry to have barged in like this. It's just that

I was in the neighbourhood. Actually, I've been asked to write Beth's official biography and I wanted to know what Mark thought...'

I was out in the hall now. Mark was still in the armchair, his head turned away from us both, apparently oblivious to any conversation between us. I called out, 'Goodbye, Mark,' over my shoulder, but there was no response.

Fiona opened the front door and, still burbling apologies, I made my way down the steps as the blue door closed firmly behind me. For a moment I stood there quite bemused. Then I turned and looked back at the house. Now it seemed to me that the windows had a blank look, the slats of the Venetian blinds like the bars of a prison, the whole house indefinably threatening, sinister almost. I turned and walked slowly back to the bustle of Notting Hill, turning over in my mind what I had seen.

I was shocked at Mark's appearance and at his general disintegration and wondered what on earth it was that had turned a pleasant, intelligent boy into what seemed little better than a zombie. I was even more puzzled by Fiona Packard. The tones in which she had addressed Mark seemed far more like those of a jailer than a lover. The whole episode had been thoroughly upsetting and what I wanted more than anything else was a good strong cup of tea. But although the many restaurants of the area offered every possible kind of fashionable cuisine, that particular comfort was not available. With a sigh, I got on a bus and went home.

Chapter Eight

After seeing Mark I suddenly wanted to talk to my son. Hilda's telephone is in the hall, which is always dark and chill even at the height of summer, so that one is not tempted to linger in idle chatter. I got right down to essentials.

'Are you having proper food?' I asked.

Michael sighed heavily. 'Dear Ma,' he said, 'when you die and go to Heaven, there you will be, sitting on a cloud, worrying about whether God is eating properly.'

'Yes, well–'

'Never thinking,' Michael continued, 'that He has choirs of angels, all perfectly capable of knocking up something hot and nourishing and taking it around to Him covered over with a plate.'

'I take that as a yes,' I said. 'What about

the animals?'

'Foss was sick yesterday – and no, before you get into a flap, it was only because he got on to the worktop and stole most of the whole bowl of fish I'd cooked for him where I'd left it to cool. So, are you having fun in the great metropolis?'

'I wouldn't say *fun*, exactly. I've done some work and seen some people. I don't really know when I'll be back. In a way, everything's a bit unsettled and I need to sort a few things out while I'm here in London.'

'Have you been to any theatres?' he asked.

'No,' I said. 'I don't seem to have got around to doing any of my usual London things.'

'Well, I think you should. All work and no play... Why don't you ring some of your old chums?'

'I might. Anyway, you're all right, then?'

'Fine.'

'What have *you* been doing?'

'Oh, this and that. Just the usual round of wild parties and turning the house into an opium den while you've been away.'

I laughed. 'All right, all right, I won't ask.'

'I must say,' Michael said meditatively, 'it's been really nice not to be sharing a house with the Spanish Inquisition for a bit.'

'Well, just you look after yourself.'

'And you, Ma. Take megacare.'

'He seems to be all right,' I said to Hilda, as I went back into the room. 'I think he's coping.'

'Of course he's coping,' Hilda said. 'He's a perfectly sensible, capable boy. I've left him this house, by the way.'

'Oh, Hilda!'

'Well, you and Michael are the only relatives I have, apart from Cousin Judith, and I have every intention of outliving *her*. And you have a perfectly good house of your own.'

'It's very generous of you–'

'Not that he'll want to live here, since he seems determined to live in the provinces.' Like a true Londoner, Hilda couldn't imagine why anyone would dream of living anywhere else. 'Still, he should get a good price for it, enough to buy something pretty substantial in Taviscombe. Not,' she continued, 'that I propose dying in the immediate future. Though there is something I do want to ask you, Sheila.'

'Yes? What's that?'

'I may not, in the nature of things, outlive Tolly...'

'Of *course* I'll look after him, Hilda. You didn't need to ask.'

She gave me her small, tight smile. 'Thank you, Sheila. I knew I could rely on you.'

She looked down at Tolly, uncharacteristically peaceful, stretched out almost the full length of the sofa, and her voice softened. 'Look at him,' she said dotingly, *'lying* there!'

Several days later I had a phone call from Phoebe Walters.

'I do hope you don't mind me calling you at home like this,' she said, 'but I'm behind schedule and the mail takes so long!'

'No, that's fine,' I replied. 'What can I do for you?'

'I wondered,' she asked tentatively, 'if you have a picture of Elizabeth Blackmore that I could borrow? I've got the one on the jacket of her books, of course, but I would like to include one of her taken when she was younger, when she was writing the early books, *Pride of Former Days* and *Nothing for Reward*. I'd get it copied and then send it right back to you.'

'Yes, I'm sure I could find you something. Leave it with me and I'll see what I can do. How is the research going? I haven't been to the library for a little while. Are you finding everything you want?'

'Yes, that's all just fine.' She paused for a moment and then said, 'Have you been through all the papers yourself yet?'

'No, there's still a lot I need to do. I've sorted through the letters, just to see what's there. I haven't actually read them all. And most of the manuscripts, though there's a few files of early unpublished stuff I haven't looked at yet. Have you had a chance to investigate it?'

'A little, but I'm concentrating on the notebooks at present. There's a great deal that's pretty seminal there.'

'That's splendid,' I said. 'Right then, I'll see what I can do about the photo.'

'I really am very grateful.'

When she had rung off I got out the box file I'd brought from home, in which I'd stuffed anything relating to Beth that had come to hand – a few letters and postcards, a couple of cuttings of reviews of her books and some old photographs I'd found in the drawer of my desk. I spread the photos out and looked at them. The image of Beth as an undergraduate stared up at me.

There were three of us, Beth, Bill and me. Dick Fielding, the fourth member of the group, had taken the photograph. We were in a punt early one May morning, having stayed up all night, waiting for the dawn and the choristers on Magdalen Tower, as the picnic basket and bottles in the bottom of the punt bore witness. In the early morning chill, Beth and I had coats over our flowery summer dresses and Bill had a college scarf wound round his neck. I had my eyes screwed up against the sun and Bill was laughing at some remark of Dick's, but Beth was sitting there simply being herself. I had forgotten how self-contained she had been, even at that relatively early age. We all looked incredibly young, younger than today's nineteen-year-olds look somehow, and the old black and white photograph seemed to make the picture seem even older than it actually was, so that we might, all three of us, have belonged to a really bygone age.

I found a couple of studio portraits of Beth, taken for publicity purposes, which she had sent to me with caustic comments written on the back. 'George Eliot's younger sister! Makes me look more like a horse than ever!' and 'Do you think I should have a nose job, or would that be giving in?' I put these into an envelope with a note to

163

Phoebe. On an impulse I also included the one in the punt. I thought Phoebe might like that.

Several days later I had a call from John.

'Beth's memorial service is to be on the thirteenth, at eleven-thirty,' he said. 'It'll be in *The Times* and the *Telegraph*, but I wanted you to know first.'

'Thank you, John, that was kind of you. Where is it to be?'

'At St Anne's on Kew Green. Ralph wanted somewhere bigger and grander – he seems to be organizing everything – but I wanted St Anne's. It's our parish church, after all, and Beth used to go there, whenever she went anywhere, though, as you know, she wasn't what you'd call a regular churchgoer.'

'I'll be there, of course.'

'I was hoping we might have had lunch together afterwards, but Ralph seems very anxious to have a talk with me – some sort of business matter connected with the copyright permission or something. But we'll have lunch soon, I hope.'

'That would be lovely.' I was silent for a moment and then I asked tentatively, 'How about the children, will they be coming?'

'Well,' John spoke hesitantly, 'I can't get hold of Mark. I just seem to get the answerphone when I ring. I've dropped him a line, though. And I'm afraid Helen can't make it – exams coming up, that sort of thing, you know. Incidentally,' he continued more briskly, 'I never thanked you properly for taking those papers down to her.'

'It was so nice to see her again,' I said. 'How *are* things now? About the business, I mean.'

'I *think* we're all right, though it's early days and we aren't out of the wood yet. But, no, I hope the worst's behind us.'

Although things seemed to be getting better for him, I was still glad John hadn't asked me how I had found Helen and I certainly didn't feel able to tell him about my encounter with Mark.

I had no real expectation of finding either of them at the memorial service. I went by myself, Hilda having expressed herself vigorously and negatively on the subject, though she did offer to lend me a hat, an offer which I refused.

The church was quite full when I arrived but, as I stood hesitating in the aisle, I saw Bill North in one of the pews near the back of the church, beckoning me to join him.

'Charlotte's got chickenpox,' he said, 'so Anne couldn't come.'

I made a sympathetic, murmuring noise and, bowing my head, muttered one of those little incoherent prayers that one does on entering a church.

As I sat back in the pew and looked around me Bill said, 'Quite a good turn-out. Ralph is up there, I see, with the great and good.'

Certainly Ralph seemed to be holding court in what I thought was an unsuitable way, while John was standing beside him looking rather lost. Almost, it looked as if

Ralph was the chief mourner and John merely a subsidiary figure at the event.

The entrance of the choir and the vicar stilled the conversational noises of the congregation and I took up the elaborately printed order of service.

'Praise to the holiest in the height,' we sang and Newman's noble hymn filled the church as the organ swelled.

It was certainly a splendidly organized occasion. A well-known literary critic gave the address, a well-known actor read, 'Fear no more the heat of the sun', and a well-known opera singer sang something by Handel. The flowers were magnificent and the service lasted precisely one hour.

'Will you have lunch with me?' Bill asked. 'I haven't got to be back at the House until three-thirty.'

'Yes please, I'd like that.'

We moved up the aisle, but our progress was slow because people were waiting to sign the book at the back of the church. A voice at my elbow said, 'Mrs Malory, hi!' I turned and saw Phoebe Walters.

'Oh, hello,' I said. 'Bill, this is Dr Walters, who is writing a book about Beth.'

They shook hands and we stood for a while making polite and meaningless remarks about the service. Then Phoebe said, 'Mr North, I wonder if you could spare the time sometime to have a few words with me, about your memories of Elizabeth Blackmore. Mrs Malory has very kindly said she would have a talk with me and I'm hoping to meet with Mr Blackmore now that he's back. It will be really helpful if I can talk to as many of her friends as possible.'

'What is this book?' Bill asked. He turned to me. 'I thought you were writing the official biography.'

'Phoebe's book will be primarily a study of the novels–' I began.

Phoebe broke in. 'But I am very anxious to relate the novels to her life.'

She began to describe in some detail the scheme of her book. I was half-listening when my attention was distracted by John, who had come up behind me and was greeting me with what seemed to be relief

'Ah, Sheila, thank you so much for coming. What a crush! I mean, it's really marvellous that so many people turned up, though I suppose I shouldn't be surprised. I always forget how famous Beth was. It's just that it's been something of an ordeal... It was very good of Ralph to arrange all this, but it's really all been a bit much!' He gave me a rueful smile.

'Look, I think I told you I have to see Ralph now, but I wondered if you'd have dinner with me tomorrow evening.'

'Yes, I'd love to.'

'You're in Holland Park, aren't you, so how about making it the Singapore in Kensington High Street, that's if you like Chinese. About seven-thirty?'

'That would be fine. I love Chinese!'

'Oh, is that Bill? I must have a word with him. Bill, how good of you to come!'

Bill turned away from Phoebe and put his arm round John's shoulder.

'Are you all right? It must have been pretty harrowing for you.' They moved away and I caught snatches of conversation 'Anne's so sorry ... Charlotte ... chickenpox... Anything we can do ... you must come to dinner really *soon...*'

I signed the book and made my way out of the church into the sunshine. Kew Green looked fresh and rural in spite of all the cars parked around it and I took a deep breath to restore myself after the stuffiness of the church, with its lingering smell of incense and unusually large congregation. Phoebe was at my side again.

'Mr North was really helpful,' she said. 'He agreed to talk to me and gave me his home address. Thank you very much, Mrs Malory, for introducing us.'

'Not at all, I hope it will be helpful. How is the research going?'

'It's fine. I have to stick at it because I have only a limited time over here, but it's coming along well. If we could have that little talk. Perhaps next week, sometime?'

'Yes, I don't see why not. I'm not sure which day, though. I'll ring you.'

Bill had left the church with John and Ralph and now came over towards me.

Phoebe said, 'Thank you very much for all your help, I do appreciate it,' and went away.

'Well now,' Bill said, 'I seem to remember that there's quite a nice little place the other side of Kew Green. Let's try that.'

We crossed the main road and found the restaurant.

'It's Greek,' I said.

'So it is, I'd forgotten. Is that all right?'

'Yes, that's fine.'

The restaurant was almost empty and very quiet and peaceful.

'Well done, Bill,' I said, 'this is the perfect place to sit and talk. Lovely not to have that ghastly Muzak or those jangly folk songs they usually have in Greek places!'

Over lunch we talked mostly about old times, as I suppose one always does on these occasions.

'It must seem odd', Bill said, 'writing the

life of an old friend, someone you know so well.'

'I'm beginning to wonder just how well I did know Beth,' I said.

Bill looked at me in some surprise.

'What do you mean?'

I hadn't intended to tell Bill what I had learned from Helen, but what with the service and all our talk about the past, it somehow slipped out.

'Did you know that she was having an affair?' I asked.

'What!'

'I know. I didn't believe it at first.'

'But–' Bill looked absolutely stunned. 'But how do you know? Who told you?'

'Helen.'

'Helen!' he exclaimed. 'Did her mother tell her?'

'No, she found out by accident.'

'Who is the man, did she say?'

I shrugged. 'She doesn't know.'

'But what happened? How did she find out?'

I told him what Helen had told me about Beth and the unknown man on Hydra.

'In Greece!'

'Yes,' I said. 'Beth had been going there quite a lot in the last few years. She said she was researching a book. Come to think of it, I suppose you might call it research in a way.'

'What on earth do you mean?' Bill asked in some bewilderment.

'There's this book we found among her papers. Didn't I tell you about it? No, of course, I haven't seen you since I discovered it.'

'What sort of book?'

'Very odd,' I said. 'Quite unlike anything else she's ever written – a different style, a completely different *sort* of book, rough, raw, very powerful, but simply not Beth at all.'

'How extraordinary.' Bill looked puzzled. 'And you think this book is somehow something to do with this affair you say she was having?'

'Somehow, yes.'

'What's the book about, then?'

'Well, the heroine is definitely Beth. She's plain – you know how Beth always had this thing about her looks, though, of course, she wasn't plain at all – but sort of fascinating. And the man, who's a big industrialist, gives up everything for her, wife, family, business, everything. She becomes a kind of obsession with him. As I told you, it's highly dramatic stuff.'

'Sounds more like melodrama to me!'

'Yes, I know, it does when you try to describe it, but it's written so well!'

'So who else has seen it?' Bill asked.

'Apart from me, only Ralph. I've given John a copy, but I don't think he's had a chance to look at it yet. Besides, I feel he isn't very interested in it.'

'I see.'

'Ralph is very keen to publish it.'

Bill gave a short laugh. 'Ah. Yes, I can see that he would be. And what do you think?'

'I don't really want to.' I leaned forward

and said earnestly, 'It would somehow seem like giving away Beth's secret, if you see what I mean.'

'And will you be able to stop Ralph?'

'I think so. If I can persuade John. He holds the copyright, of course, but if I say that I'm really sure that Beth wouldn't want it published, then I think he'd listen to me, and Ralph can't do anything without John's permission.'

Bill smiled. 'Beth has a very good friend in you, Sheila.'

'Well, it seems to me that that's what a literary executor is for.'

'Actually,' Bill said slowly, 'if the man in the book is an industrialist, couldn't he be John?'

'No,' I said firmly, 'no way. The character's quite unlike John – really powerful, charismatic, even.'

Bill was silent for a while, as if trying to come to terms with what I had just told him.

'I'm sorry, Bill,' I said impulsively, 'I

shouldn't have told you.'

'No, no, I'm glad you did. It's just – well, a bit of a shock. Like you, I feel now that I didn't really know Beth at all.'

'You'll understand why I'm beginning to wonder if I *can* write this biography after all. I mean, obviously the affair was a big thing in her life, but I can't possibly mention it. And without it, I'd feel that there was a big hole – even if no one else knew that it was there.'

'Yes, I see your problem,' Bill said. 'Still, you don't have to do anything immediately, do you?'

'No, I suppose not. There's the book of short stories to be edited first. I suppose I can put it off for a while. But I'll have to face up to it in the end, Ralph will see to that.'

'He obviously wants to strike while the iron's hot!'

'I can understand it, in a way. Novelists' literary reputations – even the most distinguished – fade so quickly, their books go out of print and, unless some startling revelation is made or some new work is suddenly discovered, they simply sink into oblivion. Well, not quite oblivion. The really good writers, like Beth, will always have a faithful band of readers, their works may even be set books in exams, but gradually they are remembered only by a few enthusiasts.'

Bill looked at me quizzically. 'You paint a gloomy picture! Will the same thing happen to your works?'

'Lit crit is slightly different,' I said. 'There are fashions, of course – who reads Bradley on Shakespeare nowadays? – but, because we are involved in the whole academic business, our books survive a little longer, even if only as terrible examples of incorrect thinking!'

Bill laughed and then looked at his watch and said, 'Sorry, I have to go if I'm going to get back into Town before three-thirty – the traffic's pretty awful on Kew Bridge! Can I give you a lift anywhere?'

'No thanks,' I said. 'It's such a lovely day,

I think I might have a little walk in Kew Gardens while I'm here. I wonder what it costs to get in now? I can remember when it only used to be one old penny.'

'Right, then. Now, where are my car keys?'

We crossed the road and stood by the church in the early afternoon sunshine.

'Thank you for my lunch,' I said, 'and for talking about old times. I think I'll do what you suggest and put the biography to one side for a while.'

We hugged each other briefly. 'Keep in touch,' Bill said. 'Now that Beth has gone we're the only ones of our lot left.'

He turned away and I walked towards the gate of the Gardens, hoping that the beauties of nature might help me to find some sort of solution to my problems.

I was almost late for my dinner with John Blackmore. Just as I was about to leave, Tolly ambushed me from behind the sofa and bit me sharply in the ankle, laddering my tights so that I had to go and find a new pair. By the time I got to the restaurant I was breathless and slightly agitated. John, too, seemed not his usual self. He was polite and agreeable as usual, but his mind seemed to be elsewhere and once or twice he began a sentence as if he was about to say something important and then broke off, making some banal remark to cover up his confusion.

We ate our way through the various delicious Chinese dishes spread before us.

'Heavenly duck,' I said. 'I think it really is my favourite!'

'I got fond of Chinese food when I was doing a big construction job in Hong Kong some years ago,' John said, dexterously helping himself to more rice with his chopsticks in a way I greatly admired. 'I've always liked it, ever since.'

'It's very good for you, I believe,' I said, following his example, though with a spoon. 'It has practically no cholesterol.'

'Well, that's all right, then!'

We talked a little about the memorial

service and John said how touched he was at the number of people who had come.

'There were quite a few people I'd liked to have had a word with, but I didn't know they were there until I read the list in *The Times*,' he said.

'It was a very stressful time for you,' I said. 'Nobody could have expected you to speak to everyone.'

'No, I suppose not. It was good of them to come, though.'

We were both silent for a while and then I asked, 'So how is Helen?'

'All right, I think. I have to go down to see her soon, there's something I have to tell her–' He broke off again.

'John,' I asked, 'is something the matter?'

'The matter?'

'Is there something you want to say to me?'

He poured us both another cup of jasmine tea.

'Well, yes, there is – it's just that I don't quite know how to tell you.'

'Just say it.'

He gave me a slight smile. 'You're right. There is no easy way to say this. I'm getting married again.'

'What!'

'I don't know how I'm going to tell Helen and Mark – I mean, so soon after–'

'You mean it's going to be soon?'

'Yes, quite soon. Next month.'

'But John–' I broke off, my mind whirling with half-formed speculation. 'Who is it?' I asked.

'Sally Bannerman. My secretary.'

Sally, 'Pretty little Sally', Beth called her, 'John's little shadow'.

'I see. But must it be so soon?' I asked, already knowing the answer.

'Yes. She's expecting a child in about six weeks' time.'

I was doing the obvious arithmetic in my head, but my mind refused to believe the figures.

'So you were–'

'Yes, we were having an affair before Beth

died. For about a year, actually.'

I pushed my plate to one side. 'John, why are you telling me this?'

He looked at me pleadingly. 'I thought you ought to know. And besides – besides, I need your advice. How do I tell the children?'

'Oh, John, I don't know, I simply don't know.'

'I'd like you to understand how it was. I know there's no excuse, but ... well, you were Beth's friend. I think you have a right to know.'

'Yes?'

'Beth had been so wrapped up in her work lately – this new book seemed to have absorbed all her energy, all her thoughts, if you know what I mean. She'd been very moody, up one minute and down the next, I never knew how she'd be from one day to another. Then this business with the children not being there – she was upset over that. It seemed she had time for everyone and everything but me. I was away a lot, of course, and Sally was with me then, so I suppose it was inevitable, really–'

'You both seemed so devoted,' I said. 'A really happy couple.'

'We were – but not for a while.'

'I really don't know what to say.'

For one moment I thought of telling John about Beth and her affair, but I knew I couldn't. Not yet, anyway. Perhaps Helen would when John told her his news.

'You must tell the children as soon as possible,' I said. 'Helen is so devoted to you she is going to be absolutely devastated. And Mark–'

I told John briefly about my encounter with Mark.

'Good God!' he said. 'I had no idea. What on earth has that woman done to him?'

'I don't know,' I said. 'The set-up was so peculiar and I was so taken aback by the whole affair–'

'I must try and do *something*,' John said in a worried tone. 'But honestly, I don't know what!'

'Go and see Helen, anyway. As soon as

possible. You really must tell her. As for Mark – well, I really don't know. Make contact, somehow. That's the only advice I can offer. I'm sorry, John, I haven't been much help.'

'You have, you've pointed me in the right direction. I really will go down to Cambridge soon – next week, perhaps. And thank you, Sheila, for being understanding, for not condemning me.' I mumbled some sort of protest, but he continued. 'You have every right to disapprove of what I've done – you were Beth's friend and it's only natural that you should feel that I've betrayed her.'

I sipped a little of my now-cold jasmine tea, feeling embarrassed and somehow hypocritical, knowing what I did about Beth's own disloyalty.

'It was really rather awful,' I told Hilda when I got back. 'There I was knowing these things about both of them – things, I may say, I'd much rather *not* have known! Oh dear, what a dreadful muddle. Those poor children! It's Helen I feel so sorry for. This will be really shattering for her. She worships John. I think she thought that with Beth gone they'd be closer than ever. And now to have a new, young stepmother, someone who'd been having an affair with her father for so long–'

'What about Mark?' Hilda asked. 'How will he take it?'

'Judging by the confused state he was in when I saw him, I don't know if he's capable of taking it in.'

'As you say, a dreadful muddle. I really cannot understand how people can lead such untidy lives.'

'I suppose they get swept away by emotions,' I said. 'Love and all that.'

'When I was young,' Hilda said repressively, 'there was such a thing as self-restraint. Now everyone – not just the young – seems to believe that whatever they want they must have, whatever the consequences to others.'

I was glad not to have to comment on this

pronouncement. Tolly was bellowing out-side the door and, when he was let in, leaped on to Hilda's lap and began to knead her skirt with his claws.

'Actually,' I said, 'I think that all this has more or less decided me. I really *don't* feel I can write that biography now. Leaving out all this would be a sort of lie and there's no way I would put it in.'

'You'd better not let Ralph learn anything about these things,' Hilda said drily. 'It would be just up his street – sensational revelations – think of all the copies *that* would sell.'

'Yes, indeed. Oh dear!' A thought struck me. 'He's bound to put two and two together when John gets married, especially after the baby is born so soon.'

'You will just have to be strong and stand your ground.'

'Yes, I suppose so. But it won't be easy.'

Tolly had jumped down from Hilda's knee and was now stalking a spider with great concentration.

'Actually, what I'll do is, I'll suggest to Phoebe Walters that she increases the biographical side of *her* book, concentrating more on the influence of Beth's life on her books. She seems reasonably scholarly, not a sensation hunter. I think it might answer quite well. I'd have to have the final say-so, but I don't suppose she'd mind that, not if I gave her permission to use all the material I would have used myself. And,' I continued with some enthusiasm, as an idea struck me, 'Ralph could publish it over here (I think she has an American publisher) so he'll still make money, so *everyone* will be happy!'

'Well, if you think she's capable of doing it properly,' Hilda said, 'and if you have the right of veto over anything at all controversial, I don't see why it shouldn't work out reasonably well. Tolly!' She broke off suddenly. 'Tolly, stop that at once! It's not good for you!'

But Tolly, having caught his spider, was eating it with every sign of enjoyment, his head on one side as he crunched the delicate morsel.

What with one thing and another, it was not until the following week that I got around to phoning Phoebe Walters. An unknown female voice answered and I asked for Phoebe. There was a moment's silence and then the voice asked, 'Who is calling?'

'My name is Sheila Malory.'

'Ah!' A sigh of what sounded like relief at the other end. 'Ah, Mrs Malory, I was on the point of calling you.'

'Calling me?' I echoed.

'Yes. I'm afraid Phoebe's had an accident.'

'Oh dear, I'm so sorry,' I said. 'Is it serious?'

'Well, yes. The fact is, she's dead.'

Chapter Nine

'Dead! Whatever happened?'

'She was knocked down by a van and she was dead when the ambulance arrived. It seems to have been a hit and run thing. Someone on the far side of the Common saw a large van driving off at speed, but they didn't actually see the accident. The police are still looking for whoever did it.'

'What a dreadful thing! When did it happen?'

'Two days ago, on Ealing Common. It was early evening but still light, the driver must have seen her. As I say, the police are still sorting things out, so we don't know very much about it yet. It's been an awful shock.'

'It must have been,' I said. 'I'm sorry, I'm afraid I don't know your name.'

'Oh, sorry, I'm Nicola Fairbairn. My

friend Nancy Bevan and I shared a flat with Phoebe.'

'It must have been very distressing for you both.'

'As I said, I was going to ring you and let you know what had happened. I mean, Phoebe told us that you'd lent her some photos or something, so I thought we ought to return them to you. Shall I put them in the post?'

'No.' I thought for a moment. 'No, if it's all right with you, I'll come and collect them. And perhaps, if no one minds, I'd like to have a look at the notes Phoebe had made for her book on Beth Blackmore. Would that be possible, do you think?'

'I don't see why not. I shouldn't think Phoebe would have minded and there's no one else now–'

'What about her relations?' I asked. 'In America, I mean.'

'Her parents were divorced,' Nicola said. 'I don't think she saw much of them. There's a brother. I found an address for him and let him know what had happened. I think he's coming over. It's all very awkward–'

'Had you known Phoebe long?'

'No, not at all. She answered an advert we put in the *Evening Standard* for someone to share the flat. She turned up and we quite liked her, so she moved in. We didn't see all that much of her. Nancy and I are out at work all day and' – she laughed – 'we lead a pretty full social life.'

'When would it be convenient for me to come?' I asked.

'Well, tomorrow's Saturday – would tomorrow morning be all right? About eleven o'clock? We should be up by then!'

'That would be fine.'

'Do you know how to get here?'

'Yes, that's all right. I had a great-aunt once, who lived in Gunnersbury Avenue, so I know the way.'

As I got out of the tube at Ealing Common, a whole lot of childhood memories came flooding back, of visits with my parents to my mother's Aunt Beatrice. She was a formidable woman who, determined to cultivate her likeness to Queen Victoria (a likeness people often remarked upon), dressed exclusively in black with touches of lace and heavy jet ornaments. When I knew her, her husband had long since departed this life ('Died young,' my father said, 'and glad to,') and, apart from her servants, the only person she had on whom to exercise her authority was a downtrodden second cousin, who had been summoned from an obscure part of Shropshire to take up the thankless position as her companion and slave.

My brother and I were greatly in awe of Great-Aunt Beatrice, not only because of her great age and autocratic manner, but also because in our childish minds we had identified her with the witch in Hansel and Gretel (something to do, no doubt, with her witch-like nutcracker nose and chin, just like the illustration in our fairy-tale book) and were in constant dread in case she felt inclined to exercise her magic powers.

I made a slight detour to walk past the house and found, sadly, though without surprise, that it had been turned into flats and that there were a number of cars parked outside in what had once been the neatly gravelled drive. A man, engaged in the ritual Saturday morning task of washing one of these cars, looked at me curiously as I stood there conjuring up the ghosts of my past, so I turned away and retraced my steps to the road leading from the Common in which Phoebe had lived.

It was a three-storied Victorian terraced house, which had a small paved area at the front with several planters full of flowers hiding a collection of dustbins, and a flight of steps leading up to the front door. I pressed the bell marked Fairbairn, Bevan, Walters and a girl in her late twenties opened the door.

'Hello. I'm Sheila Malory.'

'Oh, great. Do come in. I'm Nicola Fairbairn. Do you mind coming into the kitchen? We each have our own bed-sit and use the kitchen as a sort of communal space.'

She led the way into a large, pleasant room, comfortably cluttered, with a kitchen table covered with a dark red chenille cloth, four wooden chairs and a large dresser full of bright crockery filling one wall.

'Will you have some coffee? I've just made some. Nancy isn't up yet – a heavy night last night!'

'Coffee would be lovely, thank you. I'm so sorry about Phoebe. I hardly knew her, but she seemed a very pleasant person. What a dreadful thing! Do the police have any idea what happened?'

'Well, actually, just after you rang, the Sergeant who's looking into things came round to see us. He had a few more details but nothing much. Apparently, as I told you, some man saw this van – a blue one – driving away and Phoebe lying on the ground. He didn't actually see her being run over, but he said it was obviously the van that had done it. Unfortunately he didn't get the number.'

'How *could* anyone do something like that, just to drive off and leave her?'

'Yes, the driver must have known what he'd done. I'm afraid the police don't hold out much hope of finding the man. It's a bit like looking for a needle in a haystack.'

'I suppose so.'

'One thing does puzzle me, though. Phoebe was just going out as I came in and she looked sort of agitated. I asked her if anything was the matter and she said no, she just had a bit of a headache and was going to the chemist to get something for it. She must have been knocked down on her way back.'

'So?'

'So, she was going – and coming back – the wrong way. The nearest chemist is down by Ealing Green and she went off towards Ealing Common. I saw her going down the street. And then, coming back, she was coming back as if she'd been to Ealing

Common station. It didn't occur to me at the time, what with the accident and everything, but later I wondered where she really had been. I looked in her handbag when they brought her things back and there wasn't any aspirin or any other sort of medication in there. You must think I'm just being nosy,' Nicola said defensively, 'but it really was a bit odd, don't you think?'

'Very odd indeed. Was she out long? I mean, how long was it from the time she left here until she was knocked down?'

'It can't have been much more than half an hour.'

'So she didn't take the underground anywhere?'

'No, there wouldn't have been time.'

'As you say, it is strange.' I finished my coffee and stood up. 'Do you think I could see those notes and things?'

'Yes, of course, I'll show you her room.'

We went back into the hall and Nicola opened a door at the back of the house and I went in. Phoebe had a pleasant room, not large, but with a big window looking out on to the long strip of garden. It was furnished with a bed, a chair, a chest of drawers and a desk. There was a triangular space in one corner covered by a curtain, where her clothes were hung, and an old-fashioned mantelpiece, which she had used as a bookshelf. Everything was very neat and tidy but somehow impersonal. There was nothing immediately apparent in the room that gave any indication of the sort of person its occupant had been. I went over to the mantelpiece and looked at the books. There were several of Beth's novels, *The Bell* by Iris Murdoch, Virginia Woolf's *Mrs Dalloway* and *To the Lighthouse* and, I was touched to see, a copy of my life of Ada Leverson.

'I think she kept her notes and things in the desk,' Nicola said, going over to it and lifting the flap. 'Yes, there's a lot of stuff here, if you'd like to look at it. I'll leave you to it. Come through to the kitchen when you've finished.'

Phoebe had kept her notes as tidily as she had kept her room. There were extracts from Beth's letters and notebooks arranged in chronological order, together with brief summaries of some of the stories. There was also a plan of the book as she intended to write it, with headings and a list of people to be interviewed.

It was a thoroughly professional piece of work and I was sad to think that it would never be completed, especially since, judging by the plan, it would have been a perfectly acceptable substitute for the biography I now felt I couldn't write.

I gathered up the notes and the photographs and went out to find Nicola.

'Do you think it would be all right if I took these notes with me for a bit?' I asked.

'I don't see why not,' she said. 'I suppose I ought to give them to her brother when he comes, but if you want to borrow them until then–'

'Oh, I only want them for a few days, I'll get them back to you by the end of next week. When is her brother coming?'

'On Wednesday, I think.' She paused. 'I don't quite know what he wants to do about the funeral, if he wants it to be here or what.'

'Yes, of course, it must be so awkward for you. I suppose there might have to be an inquest?'

'I suppose so.' She got up and went over to the stove. 'Would you like another cup of coffee?'

'No thanks, I must be going.' I gathered up my handbag and put the papers in my shopping bag. 'Actually, I wonder if you could do something for me?'

'Of course, if I can.'

'Would you mind walking across the Common and showing me where the accident happened?'

Nicola looked a little surprised by this request. 'Yes,' she said. 'Just a minute while I get a jacket. I'd better let Nancy know I'm going out.'

As we walked up to the Common, Nicola

said, 'It was at this far end, by Elm Avenue, away from the main road. As you can see, there isn't a proper pavement here, so she'd have been walking on the grass or on the road.'

I looked across the expanse of the Common, lined with chestnut trees and bisected by short roads. Since it was Saturday morning there were quite a few people about, children playing, cars parked on the side roads, but even at such a relatively busy time such as this there weren't any people about at this end.

'It was here.' Nicola stopped. 'Just by the corner. You can see the tyre marks. It had been raining that day so the ground was muddy, but it hasn't rained since.'

'The marks go right over the edge and on to the grass,' I said. 'That's odd.'

'I believe the police think it was a drunken driver,' Nicola said. 'That's what the Sergeant implied. They think he lost control going round the corner and swerved right into her.' She shuddered. 'It really is awful, when you think about it.'

'I'm sorry,' I said, 'I shouldn't have asked you–'

'No, that's all right.'

'It's not just morbid curiosity,' I said. 'I just wanted to get it clear in my mind, what happened. Thank you very much for everything. I'll get the notes back to you in a few days. Oh, by the way, could you let me know when Phoebe's brother arrives? I'd like to have a word with him.'

'Poor girl,' Hilda said when I told her where I had been. 'It really was the most unlucky accident. A one in a million chance.'

'So now I'm back to square one,' I said. 'And I know I'm being selfish, but what *am* I to do about that wretched biography? Phoebe Walters would have done a perfectly adequate job.'

'There must be other suitable scholars,' Hilda said. 'You must cast your mind around.'

'Yes, I suppose so,' I said wearily. 'Oh dear,

this is all so difficult!'

'There's no point in letting it become a *burden*,' Hilda said, getting up from the lunch table and gathering up the plates. She went out into the kitchen and I followed her with the rest of the dishes. Tolly was sitting in the sink, meditatively batting with one fawn paw at the drips from the tap. Hilda lifted him out of the sink and put him gently on the floor. 'Who's a beautiful boy, then?' she enquired. Tolly gave her a scornful look and walked meaningfully over to his dish, waiting to be placated with food.

'You're right,' I said, 'I need a change of scene. Let's go and look at that new exhibition that's just opened at the British Museum.'

It was a good exhibition, though exhaustingly large.

'I really don't think I can take any more in,' I said. 'I'm getting mental indigestion. Do you mind if we abandon the last couple of rooms?'

'I do feel that some thought might be

given', Hilda said, 'to the proportion of seats to the number of the exhibits. There is virtually nowhere to sit down. Yes, I think a gin and tonic would round things off nicely.'

'I think we might go to the pub round the corner,' I said. 'As it's Saturday I don't think I'm in any danger of seeing Ralph Hastings in there this time. He's the *last* person I want to meet at the moment!'

We had settled into a corner with our drinks and were poring over the exhibition catalogue – in my case finding all sorts of important things I'd missed – when a voice behind me said, 'Mrs Malory! I do hope you don't mind my bothering you like this, but I've been meaning to write to you.'

I looked up and saw Rachel Edwards, the girl from the Senate House Library.

'No, of course not,' I said. 'Do sit down. What will you have to drink?'

'No, nothing thanks. I'm with someone, actually, but when I saw you over here, I thought I'd take the opportunity to have a few words.'

'Right then, what can I do for you?'

She sat down opposite me and for a moment seemed unsure of how to begin. Then she suddenly plunged in. 'Mrs Malory, I think one of the documents in the Beth Blackmore papers has been stolen.'

Chapter Ten

For a moment I didn't really take in what Rachel was saying and then Hilda said sharply, 'What exactly do you mean, stolen? Please explain.'

This brusque command seemed to have a bracing effect on Rachel because she said, 'I only discovered it yesterday and I've been in specially today to check and recheck to make sure I wasn't mistaken–'

'Yes, yes,' Hilda said impatiently, 'but *what* is missing?'

'It's the carbon copy of some notes for one of the novels.'

'A carbon?'

'Yes,' I said. 'Beth always used a type-writer, she couldn't be doing with computers and word processors.' I turned to Rachel. 'Are you sure that's what it was?'

'Yes, I checked it with the accessions record. As I say, it was the carbon of the notes Beth Blackmore made for *How Like a Winter*. About ten pages – the original's still there.'

'But who,' I asked in some bewilderment, 'would want to steal *that*? I mean, it's not as though any of Beth's manuscripts would fetch some enormous amount on the open market! Are you sure it isn't just misplaced?'

Rachel shook her head. 'No, really, I've checked everywhere. It's the most awful thing to have happened. I don't know what Miss Williams is going to say!'

She seemed to shrink in her seat and looked more mouse-like than ever.

'Well,' I said bracingly, 'it doesn't seem to be a matter of life and death, especially if we've still got the original.'

'But it's the *principle!*' Rachel said earnestly. 'The fact that *anything* could be taken like that.'

'I still can't imagine what anyone would want to take it *for*,' I said. 'It really is quite bizarre. Who's been looking at the papers, anyway?'

'Only the people you gave permission to,' Rachel said. 'There was Dr Walters, of course, and those two other Americans, from the University of Chicago I think they were.'

'Oh yes, they're doing some sort of anthology.'

'And a young man from South Africa and one from Leeds.'

'Yes, I remember them, but they seemed perfectly responsible from their letters.'

'I think that was all. Oh no, there was someone called Ralph Hastings. I think you said he was her publisher. He was in the other day.'

'Yes, of course, he did ask me if he could have a look at what was there. But *he* wouldn't want to steal anything!'

'Have you seen these notes?' Hilda asked me.

'No, actually, I haven't. I suppose I'd better go in on Monday and have a look at the original and see why anyone would want to steal it.' I turned to Rachel. 'Anyway, don't you worry about it. I know you must have looked after the papers most conscientiously. I'll have a word with Miss Williams on Monday. You go off and enjoy yourself with your friends!'

'Thank you very much, Mrs Malory. I'm really sorry it happened.' She gave me her polite little smile and got up. I saw her joining a fair-haired young man in a blue anorak, who had been watching her anxiously, and they left the pub together.

'Well,' I said, 'what an extraordinary thing!'

Janet Williams gave an exclamation of annoyance when I told her the reason for my visit.

'There is really no excuse for that sort of thing to happen,' she said.

'I'm sure it isn't Rachel's fault, she seems most efficient.'

I broke off as Janet opened the door of the

ancient lift and more or less held my breath as we completed the jerky ascent. Rachel produced the box the papers should have been in, and then various other boxes, until Janet had satisfied herself that they really weren't there.

'Well, it is most annoying,' she said. 'I shall have to make a report.'

'Do you have to?' I asked. 'I mean, it is only a carbon and I don't mind and I'm sure John won't want any sort of fuss—'

'It's procedure,' Janet said firmly and went away, presumably to make her report.

I sat down with the original of the document and prepared to examine it thoroughly to see what, if anything, made it worth stealing. Beth had taken the theme of absence from the Shakespeare sonnet, which she had copied out at the head of her notes. The book was set in the Second World War and dealt with the life of a woman whose husband was a prisoner of war.

I turned over the pages of the notes. There were a lot of factual details about the war –

shortages, war news, the food people ate, the clothes they wore, radio programmes and so forth – and brief sketches of the subsidiary characters, their jobs and the places they lived. The main characters were dealt with in more detail, with full biographies, physical descriptions and lists of their predominant characteristics. The plot was set out chapter by chapter and the whole thing was an impressive exercise in discipline and control. Actually, Beth once told me that although she quite enjoyed working out what she called the schedule of a new novel, she often jettisoned it halfway through if some strand of the story, or some especially powerful character, took her interest. But I could find nothing in the whole thing that would make it worth stealing.

I turned back to the sonnet. There was a faint pencil mark in the margin beside two of the lines:

For Summer and his pleasures wait on thee,

And, thou away, the very birds are mute:

It was, of course, the theme of the book, but did those lines have a more personal significance for Beth? The book was written five or six years ago and I somehow didn't feel that those lines had any connection with her feelings for John, so had her affair already been going on that long ago? I closed the box with a sigh. I was, if anything, even more confused now.

'The whole thing is really *peculiar*,' I said to Hilda that evening at supper. 'Not only this missing manuscript, but everything – Beth's death, Phoebe's accident, Mark's extraordinary behaviour, not to mention Beth's affair and John's girlfriend! I mean, every time I look at anything it gets shifted off-key!'

'In spite of your oddly mixed metaphor,' Hilda said, 'I see what you mean.' She spooned some mashed potato on to her plate and passed the dish to me. 'Are you suggesting that all these things are in some way related?'

'I don't know. It almost seems as if they might be, but how?'

'Consider the facts clearly, in chronological order.'

'Well, first of all there's Beth's death – no, hang on, Mark was behaving oddly *before* that. So, first there's Mark's strangeness, which seems to have something to do with that Fiona person, *then* Beth dies, then we find out about her affair with whoever–'

'Just a minute,' Hilda interrupted me. 'Don't forget about John Blackmore's financial troubles.'

'Yes, I suppose so. Right, there's that and Helen giving him her share of Beth's money, then we hear about John's affair and the baby – but *Helen* doesn't know about that, at least not then – then Phoebe is knocked down and killed and now this manuscript has gone missing. Well!' I looked at Hilda. 'What do you make of all that?'

Hilda was silent for a moment. Then she

said slowly, 'I suppose it might all fit together if Beth's death wasn't an accident.'

'What do you mean?'

'Consider the facts in a new light. John had a mistress he wanted to marry and he was also about to be plunged into severe financial difficulties. He needed Beth's money but, of course, if she knew about this girl, he wouldn't get it.'

'Yes, I'm with you so far.'

'Helen adored her father and hated her mother for deceiving him (not, of course, knowing about *his* unfaithfulness). She might have known about John's financial problems and decided to solve them in her own way.'

'What about Phoebe and the missing manuscript?'

'It is possible that Phoebe somehow found out that Beth's death wasn't an accident and had to be silenced.'

'And the manuscript?'

'I don't know,' Hilda admitted, 'unless there was something in it that you've missed that gave Phoebe a clue about what had happened.'

'Well,' I said doubtfully, 'it's a theory, I suppose. But I still don't see how Beth *could* have been murdered. I mean, how could someone have persuaded her to take those tablets together, when she knew it would be dangerous?'

'The second lot could have been ground up and put in her food,' Hilda said. 'There are all sorts of ways it could be done. And we don't *know* that she was on her own at that cottage.'

'I suppose not,' I agreed reluctantly. 'It's quite isolated, the last cottage at the end of a lane. No one would have seen someone come and go. Oh, I don't know. Now I'm *really* confused.'

Hilda began to gather up the plates. 'It's gooseberries and custard for pudding,' she said. 'I put a pinch of bicarbonate of soda in the gooseberries. It takes away the acidity.'

The following day something happened that

seemed, uncannily, to confirm at least part of our theory. I had a phone call from Nicola.

'Mrs Malory?' Her voice sounded strained. 'I thought I'd better let you know. The police have been round. They've found a van abandoned somewhere in Hammersmith. They think it's the one that knocked down Phoebe.'

'How do they know?' I asked.

'Blood, I think, and fragments of clothing embedded in the dented paintwork.'

'Good heavens!'

'So they're treating it as a suspicious death and want to look at all her things. Could you possibly let me have those papers back in case they want to see them?'

'Yes, of course. I'll bring them round. Would tomorrow evening be all right? When will you be in?'

'About sevenish, if that's all right for you.'

'Yes, that's fine. I'll see you then.'

Hilda was out, so I couldn't tell her about the latest development.

'It really is very strange, though,' I said out loud as I put the phone down. Tolly, who was sleeping stretched out at full length on the sofa, raised his head, regarded me with a blank, blue stare and put his chin back on his paws.

I suddenly realized that I hadn't looked at all of Phoebe's notes that I'd brought away with me. I opened the folder and began to sort through them. Suddenly I gave an exclamation which startled Tolly into raising his head again. There, among the other papers, was the missing carbon. I took it out and looked at it carefully. It was exactly the same as the original. There were not, as I had half-imagined, any pencilled notes or comments that might have made it in some way significant. The only thing that was different was a mark which indicated that the pages had been stapled together, but what, if anything, that meant, I had no idea.

It was raining when I left the underground station, so I put my umbrella up and hurried across Ealing Common, doing no more than cast a quick glance at the corner where Phoebe was run down. Nicola looked very serious when she greeted me at the front door of the flat.

'There's been another development,' she said. 'Do come in and get dry. Will you have coffee or will you have a glass of wine?'

'Wine would be nice,' I said gratefully. 'Oh, white, please, that's lovely. Thank you. So what's happened?'

'They sent a CID man round,' Nicola said, 'a Sergeant Mortimer. He said that it does look as if Phoebe's death wasn't an accident at all. I told you that they found this van?' I nodded. 'Well, when they examined it they found that all the fingerprints – on the doors and the wheel and so forth – had been wiped clean.'

'Good heavens!'

'Yes. And, when they checked the registration, they discovered that the dealer sold it to someone who paid for it in cash and gave a false name and address.'

'How extraordinary!' Where was this dealer?'

'Not a proper dealer, really. Just some little backstreet garage in Acton.'

'Who'd be used to cash deals and no questions asked?'

'I think so, it was that sort of garage.'

'Did the police get a description of the man who bought it?' I asked.

'Not really. Average height, just ordinary looking. Wearing jeans, a bomber jacket and a baseball cap. Not very young, the man said, and with a North Country accent. Geordie, he thought. But he was pretty vague. I got the impression he was known to the police anyway and he seemed nervous and didn't want to get involved. There may have been something not right about the van, I don't know. So that's the only description the police have to go on. Not much, really!'

'Why on earth would this man want to kill Phoebe?' I asked. 'Come to that, why would *anyone* want to kill Phoebe?'

Nicola shook her head. 'I can't imagine,' she said. 'It's all beyond me!'

'Did she have a boyfriend?' I asked.

'Not that I know of. Not over here, at any rate. I suppose there may have been someone in the States. I could ask her brother.'

'Oh, is he here?'

'Yes, he arrived yesterday. He's staying in Phoebe's room – London hotels are so expensive!'

'I expect he was very upset,' I said.

'Yes and no,' Nicola replied. 'Upset as you would be to hear about the death of a friend, say, but not upset enough for the death of a sister, if you see what I mean.'

'You feel that they didn't get on?' I asked.

'Well, certainly not close, I should think. Apparently, when the parents divorced, Phoebe went with the mother, but Ben (that's the brother) went to live with his father. So I suppose they didn't see each other that much.'

'I see.'

'The whole thing is so *peculiar*,' Nicola said. 'I mean, it seems such an odd way to kill someone.'

'It appears to have been very effective,' I said.

'You could say that.'

'What was Phoebe like?' I asked. 'I only met her a couple of times, but she seemed quite a pleasant girl.'

Nicola hesitated for a moment. 'It's not really easy to say,' she said slowly. 'Actually, we saw very little of her. She was out quite a lot – at the library, I think – and then when she was here she was mostly in her room working. She said she had a deadline, that is, she only had a limited time over here to do her research.'

'You didn't have any sort of social contact at all, then?'

Nicola shrugged. 'Not really. We met in the kitchen in the mornings. She didn't seem to eat breakfast, she only had coffee. And in the evenings she didn't cook for herself. She either went out to get something – locally, I think – or brought in a pizza or a take-away.'

'No visitors?'

'No, not that I ever saw. No, she seemed to be just an ordinary sort of girl.'

'The only thing is', I said, 'that she took – I don't know if you could call it stealing, she may have meant to put it back – a document from the library. I found it among these papers that I took away to have a look at.'

'No! What an extraordinary thing! Why would she steal something like that? Was it valuable?'

'No,' I said. 'Not at all. In fact, it was a carbon of a document that's still there. There seems to be no earthly reason for anyone to take it. But, because it's such an odd thing, I can't help wondering if it had something to do with her murder. I suppose we must call it murder now.'

'But–' Nicola looked at me in bewilderment. 'But what could be the connection? I mean, if the document is just a copy of another–?'

'I honestly haven't a clue,' I said. 'But it's the only really odd thing we know about her. I suppose the police ought to know.'

'I suppose so—'

She was interrupted by a knock on the kitchen door. A young man put his head round the door and said, 'May I come in?'

He was obviously Phoebe's brother. He had the same colouring and the same dark, curly hair.

'Oh yes, of course,' Nicola said. 'Come in, Ben. This is Sheila Malory, who knew Phoebe slightly.'

'I'm Elizabeth Blackmore's literary executor,' I explained. 'I gave Phoebe permission to look at some documents in the Senate House Library. We only met quite briefly a couple of times.'

'Pleased to meet you.'

'Will you have a glass of wine?' Nicola asked.

'It's very kind of you, but would you mind if I had a coffee instead?' He moved over to the stove, where the percolator was bubbling away and poured himself a cup.

'This must have been a dreadful shock for you,' I said formally.

'Well, yes, I guess it was. As Nicola here will tell you, I hadn't had much to do with Phoebe for a while, but yes, it was quite a shock.'

'The police', I said, probing a little, 'appear to think it wasn't an accident – that it was murder.'

'Yes, I saw the Sergeant. He told me.'

'It seems such an extraordinary thing. Can you think of anyone who might want to kill her?'

He shrugged. 'No, but then, as I said, I haven't been in touch with her for a while.'

'She seemed a perfectly nice, ordinary girl,' I said.

He hesitated for a moment and then he said, 'Well, perhaps not nice.'

Nicola and I exchanged glances. 'What do you mean?' she asked.

'Well–' Having made this statement, he seemed reluctant to continue. 'What is it they say about not speaking ill of the dead? But Phoebe *wasn't* what you'd call nice. She was selfish and manipulative, greedy too, wanted whatever life could offer and not too worried about how she got it.' He took a sip of his coffee and regarded us with a slightly defensive air. 'I know, I know, I'm her brother, I shouldn't be saying these things, but they're true. When our parents were splitting up, Phoebe used to play one off against the other, so that they'd be vying with each other for her affection, buying her things, you know, that kind of stuff. She was only a kid then, twelve years old, but she knew how to get things out of them. Then, when the divorce came, she chose to go with my mother, who had this rich new boyfriend, rather than to stay with Dad, who was more or less cleaned out financially by the settlement. It pretty well broke his heart—'

His voice trailed away and he was silent.

'I'm so sorry,' I said.

'To be honest,' Ben went on, 'I only came

over when Nicola here told me about Phoebe being killed because my father asked me to.'

'Yes, I see.' I hesitated for a moment and then I went on, 'I wasn't going to tell you, but after what you've just said... Actually, it seems that Phoebe took some documents from the Senate House Library.'

'Stole them, you mean?'

'Well, yes.'

'Were they valuable?' Ben asked.

'No, that's what's so odd. I mean, there was nothing special or important about them at all.'

Ben frowned. 'There must have been something in it for her. Phoebe never did anything without a reason.'

'Oh well,' I said. 'We'll probably never know now.'

I turned to Nicola. 'Perhaps you could tell the police. See if they think it's important.'

'Yes, of course.'

'Are you staying over here for long?' I asked Ben.

'For a little while,' he said.

'Ben's staying until after the inquest,' Nicola said. 'The police haven't released the body, so there can't be a funeral yet. Ben's father wants him to take the ashes back to Philadelphia.'

It seemed to me that her tone was protective and certainly Ben gave her a warm smile when she said, 'Anyway, he might as well see something of London while he's here.'

'Nicola's been very kind,' he said, 'showing me around and letting me stay here.'

'I think they're both rather attracted to each other,' I said to Hilda that evening. 'So perhaps something good may come out of all this.'

'She knows nothing at all about him. Really, Sheila, you are incurably sentimental,' Hilda said austerely.

'He seems a very nice young man,' I said defensively.

'You thought this Phoebe girl was nice,' Hilda reminded me, 'but now it turns out that she was no such thing.'

'Yes, that was very odd,' I admitted. 'She seemed such a nice girl, but I suppose she was being nice because she wanted something out of me. And anyway, Americans have such good manners. I suppose that was why I was deceived.'

'Well,' Hilda said, 'she must have done something fairly drastic to get herself killed.'

'Yes, but *what*? I really can't think of anything.'

'Perhaps she knew something that might have been dangerous to another person. Suppose for a moment,' Hilda went on, warming to her theme, 'that Beth *was* murdered. Might there have been something in her papers, the ones in the Senate House Library, that might have been incriminating in some way? Phoebe had been going over them for a little while, hadn't she?'

'I really don't know,' I said. 'I haven't been

through them all myself, so I can't really say *exactly* what's there. I suppose there could be something. But there wasn't anything in the papers she stole—'

'Forget those,' Hilda said, 'they're probably just some things she took to work on at home. She obviously wasn't too scrupulous about how she went about things. No, say she found a letter or something that made her suspect that Beth hadn't died a natural death, that someone had a motive to kill her. Now, from what her brother said, she was not the sort of person who would stop at blackmail.'

'And you think whoever she was blackmailing killed her?'

'It seems the only possible explanation.'

'But we haven't any evidence that Beth was murdered.'

'True. I am only putting it forward as a hypothesis. But supposing she was, then, as we have considered before, there were several people who might either wish her death or profit by it.'

'It sort of comes back to John, doesn't it?' I said sadly.

'Certainly his motive is the strongest.'

'But what on earth could there have been in the papers that might make Phoebe think he had murdered Beth?'

'Beth was a writer and was, I believe, in the habit of making notes and observations for her novels. Perhaps,' Hilda said drily, 'Beth had sketched out a scenario which involved an unfaithful husband, desperately needing money from his rich wife.'

'It's a possibility, certainly,' I agreed. 'And Phoebe put two and two together and tried to blackmail John and he killed her.'

'It is the only possible explanation I can think of.'

'I shall have to tell John about Phoebe's death,' I said. 'I suppose I could try and find out, in a roundabout sort of way, where he was when she was killed. It won't be easy!'

Chapter Eleven

But all thoughts of Phoebe's death were driven out of my head the next day by a telephone call I had from Arnold's friend Alex.

'Sheila, my dear, I have to telephone to you at this most peculiar time because it is when Arnold is out and it is to be the surprise for him. For his seventieth birthday I am making a party and I wish you will come.'

'Oh, Alex–'

'Now do not say no! It will be too sad if you are not there, now that there will be no Beth.'

'Well, I'd love to come, of course, but–'

'No buts, Sheila, you will come. Lisa and Guido are coming from Milan and Basil and Felipe from Alexandria, so there will

231

not be room at the apartment, but I will book you a room at that most nice Athenian Inn, which you like and which is so very near. Now that is settled. It is next week. The party is on Tuesday – Arnold's birthday – so you will come on Monday–'

'Will there be anyone else coming from England?' I asked.

'I asked Bill – Bill North – but he is busy with some tiresome political thing. And John is away. His secretary said for a week. So you see, Sheila, you must come or Arnold will be so disappointed to have no one from his past. No?'

'It's very short notice,' I protested.

'But it was a – what do you call it? – a spur-of-the-moment thing. I only decide yesterday and so it must be!'

'Oh, all right, then,' I said submitting to the inevitable, as one always does with Alex. 'Book me a room for the Monday and Tuesday, then.'

'You should stay longer – have a little holiday.'

232

'I'll have to stay Tuesday night to get over the party!'

'That is excellent. You will see, it will be the most fabulous party. I have invited Ion – you remember him, so attractive a young man, and Dr Pemberton, from the British Institute, who also admires you. And I have planned the most *delicious* food, you will be ravished!'

'Oh dear,' I said to Hilda, 'I can't imagine why I let myself in for something like this, it will be so exhausting!'

'Nonsense. It will do you good. Stop you brooding about this Beth and Phoebe business. Anyway, you haven't had a holiday for a very long time.'

'I went up to Kirkby Lonsdale to stay with Joan at Easter,' I said.

'I wouldn't call that a holiday,' Hilda said. 'Joan is very *demanding* nowadays. I can't imagine you had a very restful time.'

'Well, no, not restful exactly,' I said, 'but she's very entertaining and the countryside up there is very beautiful. Anyway, I seem to have committed myself to this Greek trip so I suppose I'd better see if I can get a flight.'

Hilda was right, of course, it did do me good to get away. I love Athens, smog and all, and I felt a lift of the spirits as Alex drove me from the airport to my hotel.

'The party tomorrow is in the evening and the others I meet at the airport in the afternoon,' he said, 'but you will come for a lunch – you will be the first surprise.'

I had an early supper – well, eight o'clock, which is early for Athens – at a little restaurant I always used to go to with Peter, where, to my great delight, they still insist on serving toast with everything, seeming to feel that it is a mark of great sophistication. The next morning I walked down to the square and sat at one of the cafés, watching the people and just enjoying being somewhere so splendidly foreign, until it was time to go to lunch.

Arnold was gratifyingly surprised and

pleased to see me.

'Sheila! My dear! This is a wonderful birthday treat.'

'It's lovely to see you, Arnold, you really haven't changed a bit. I can't believe you're seventy.'

'My dear, please do not remind me. Three score years and ten is so *biblical*, practically Old Testament.' Now let us have some delicious ouzo. I have found a new one that is *immensely* strong.'

I declined the ouzo, having painful memories of some of Arnold's previous 'finds', but accepted a glass of white wine instead.

'It is so good to see you,' Arnold said, pouring a little water into his own glass and watching the liquid become viscous and milky, 'especially now that poor Beth has gone.' There were tears in his eyes and I laid a hand on his arm. 'How could it have happened?' he demanded. 'It was such an unnecessary tragedy. Why was there no one there?'

'She was at the cottage, by herself,' I said. 'She'd gone there to work on her new book.'

'Ah, yes, the Greek book.' He sighed. 'And now it will never be written. Such a loss. She worked so hard here, so much research, it was going to be a masterpiece.'

Alex got to his feet and said, 'There is lunch for you both, all ready. Me, I have to go out now and prepare the next surprise. I will tell you what it is. More guests for you, Arnold – Lisa and Guido and Basil and Felipe. I am meeting them soon at the airport. They are coming for a big party, for you, tonight. They are staying here, which is why Sheila here is at the Athenian Inn. Now I go and leave you to have lunch and to gossip a little, which you will enjoy.'

Arnold gave an exclamation of surprise. He turned to me and said, 'Did you know about this?'

'Of course,' I said, 'that's why I'm here!'

Alex went away and we went into the kitchen and sat down to the dish of roast lamb, garlic and new potatoes.

'This is absolutely heavenly,' I said. 'I really must get the recipe from Alex. I've tried several times to make it from memory, as it were, but it never turns out right!'

'So,' Arnold said, pouring wine into my glass and topping up his ouzo, 'Beth's Greek book was never started?'

'There were some notes,' I said, 'among her papers. Did you know that she made me her literary executor?'

'An excellent appointment,' Arnold said. 'You will be faithful to her wishes.'

'Actually,' I said, 'Ralph – you know, Ralph Hastings, her publisher – wants me to write her biography.'

He nodded gravely. 'A great responsibility,' he said, 'but I am sure you will make a splendid job of it.'

'That's just it, Arnold. I don't think I can do it.'

He looked at me in some surprise. 'Why ever not? You are a good biographer, you were a friend of Beth and knew her well, and you have, presumably, access to all her papers. What is the problem?'

'But I didn't! Know her well, I mean. There were things about her life I knew nothing about, she wasn't the person I thought.'

'What do you mean?'

I was silent for a moment and then plunged in. 'Arnold, did you know that Beth was having an affair?'

'Ah.' He leaned back in his chair and put the tips of his fingers together, as he used to do when he was about to make an important point in a tutorial. 'I see.'

'You did know?'

'Yes. That is, I knew there was someone, but I have no idea who he was. May I ask how you knew?'

'Helen told me.'

'Helen!'

'Yes,' I said. 'Poor child, she was very upset – you know how devoted she is to her father. Apparently a friend of hers saw Beth with this man on Hydra.'

'How very distressing.' Arnold looked troubled.

'It's even worse than that,' I said. I told him about John's approaching marriage and about the child. 'Helen is going to be absolutely devastated by that. It will seem to her like the ultimate betrayal. I mean, she wouldn't have anything to do with Beth, after she discovered about *her* affair – completely wiped her out of her life. But now to be told that John, as well... It really doesn't bear thinking about!'

'She is very young,' Arnold said. 'She will not understand. To the young, everything is black and white.'

'How did *you* find out? About Beth, I mean.'

'She told me.'

'Really!'

'Yes. She had been staying here with us for a while and then she went off to the islands, to do research, she said, and when she came back she was quite different. Transformed, so happy. I asked her why and she told me. But she wouldn't tell me who the man was. She said she couldn't.'

'Did she say why?' I asked curiously.

'I assumed it was because he was married too and she was being discreet.'

'What did you think about it, Arnold? Really.'

He thought for a moment and then he said, 'I was sad, I suppose. We put people on a pedestal. I thought of Beth as someone dedicated to her work, above such things.'

'But she had John and the children.'

'All that part of her life was behind her. The children were grown up and John – well, I never felt that it was a grand passion, nothing that would come between her and the really important thing in her life. She was a great writer – well, you know that – and, as such, she had a duty to her great gift, not to dissipate her energies in other ways.'

'But she was a human being as well,' I said gently.

'It is given to very few,' Arnold said, 'to achieve something really fine. That should always come first, no matter what the circumstances. And now she is dead and all those novels that she might have written will never be written. She neglected her gift and now she is dead.'

We were both silent for a while and then I said, 'But you do see, don't you, why I feel I can't write her biography?'

He nodded. 'Yes, I do.'

'And really,' I continued, 'we must be glad that she had this great happiness.'

Arnold smiled. 'Perhaps,' he said.

I left the apartment before the other guests arrived. Partly because I didn't want to be involved in the general exclamations, clamour and continental high emotion that I knew would ensue, and partly because I knew that the party wouldn't begin until very late (Athenian fashion) and I felt I needed a little lie down on my bed before I could face the festivities before me.

Actually, I slept a little and, since it took me quite a long time to make myself look elegant enough to face Arnold's friends, it was nearly ten o'clock when I arrived at the apartment.

The drawing room, though large, seemed full of people, all talking animatedly in several different languages, while smoke, curling up from pungent continental cigarettes, made the atmosphere seem even more daunting. However, Alex greeted me with great enthusiasm and Arnold received with every appearance of pleasure the books I had brought as a present for his birthday. I presently retreated from the hub, as it were, of the main activity and found myself a relatively quiet corner, from which I could sit and observe my fellow guests. I knew some of them from my previous visits, various members of the university and the British School, a few of Arnold's former students and other friends, as well as that small group of elderly ladies dressed in black with a great many diamonds, without whom no Athenian gathering of this kind is complete. I looked around the room, at the polished wooden floor, the heavy, dark-wood furniture, the exquisite handwoven rugs on the walls and the originals of the charming watercolours which decorated Arnold's elegantly written travel books, and I thought how odd it was that I should be here, part of this cosmopolitan but alien scene.

'Sheila! How delightful to see you again!' It was Cyril Pemberton, an old Oxford friend, now living and teaching in Athens. 'Alex told me you were coming.'

We sat for a while, chatting about Arnold and Athens and the old Oxford friends.

'I was so sorry,' Cyril said, 'to hear about Beth. Such a shock. Poor Arnold was devastated. I always felt that he had something of a *tendresse* for her.'

'Yes,' I replied, 'it was very sad.'

'I saw her, of course, the last time she was over here. She was only in Athens quite briefly before she went off to the islands – to do some sort of research, I believe–'

He was interrupted by the arrival of another guest. A guest, apparently of some considerable importance, since a hush fell upon the company as he entered the room, even the elderly ladies ceasing their high, bird-like chattering.

He was a large man, tall and well built, with thick grey hair brushed back from his forehead, heavy horn-rimmed glasses lending importance to an already impressive face. Arnold went forward to greet him.

'Theo! This is a very great pleasure!'

'My dear friend, the pleasure is all mine, to be here on such an auspicious occasion!'

His voice was deep and well modulated, the Athenian accent slightly overlaid by American.

Under the cover of the general conversation which had started up again, I said to Cyril Pemberton, 'Who is that?'

'That, my dear Sheila, is Theodore Andros.'

'Really!' Even I had heard of Andros, the Greek shipping magnate. He was a legend both for his business dealings and his philanthropy – several museums and libraries bore his name. Unlike some of his business rivals, he was known for the austerity of his life; he lived only in Greece and was not part of that international set whose playground is the Riviera.

'How very grand,' I said, 'to have him at one's party!'

'I think Arnold met him some years ago – something to do with the university.'

'He looks pretty formidable.'

'Oh, he is, but very charming. You'll see.'

I saw Arnold and Theodore Andros coming towards me.

'I'll leave you to it,' Cyril said and moved away.

'Sheila,' Arnold said, 'may I present Theodore Andros? Theodore, this is my dear friend Sheila Malory.'

'A friend from Oxford days, I believe,' Andros said, smiling. 'I was myself at Cambridge, but I have much respect for the Other Place.'

He bowed slightly and I inclined my head in what I hoped was a gracious acknowledgement.

'What did you read at Cambridge?' I asked.

'Officially,' he smiled again, 'officially I read economics, but I must confess I spent many hours listening to Dr Leavis talking about English literature.'

'Ah,' I said, 'so you are a Leavisite!'

'In many ways, yes, though I must confess that I part company with him in his evaluation of Jane Austen, for whom I have a positive adoration.'

'That seems very right and proper,' I said.

'When I am in England I go always to Chawton to make my pilgrimage, and also to Bath – though she disliked it, I know – but it is still so much her place. When I am there I always carry an umbrella like Captain Wentworth! I believe *Persuasion* is my favourite of the novels. Arnold tells me that you live near to Bath. Next time I am in England perhaps you will permit me to call upon you?'

'That would be delightful,' I replied, trying to imagine the impact of an internationally famous Greek shipping magnate on Taviscombe society.

'And perhaps we could, together, fulfil my great ambition, to visit Lyme Regis. Is that correct, or do you say simply Lyme? English place names are so idiosyncratic, are they not?'

'No,' I said, 'Lyme Regis is perfectly correct.'

'Then that is settled. Next year, we will walk together on the Cobb.'

'I will look forward to it,' I said.

He bowed slightly and then he said suddenly, 'Poor Beth, we talked much of English literature. She was a great writer, perhaps one of the greatest this century, even Dr Leavis must have admitted as much, do you not agree? You were her friend, were you not? And Arnold says you are her literary executor.'

'Yes, I am.'

'I am sure she could not have chosen a more suitable person. It is so tragic, her early death. She had so much still to do.'

'I still can't really believe that she is dead.'

'I too feel this.' He nodded his head gravely. 'And what will your duties be, as a literary executor?'

'Well, I'm still sorting through her papers, her notebooks and so forth. I've more or less edited a selection of her short stories for the press and I've been asked to write her official biography.'

'Really? And will you do that?'

I sighed. 'I really don't know. I was quite keen at first, but then, oh, various things happened that made me wonder just how well I knew Beth, how qualified I am to write about her life—'

'Indeed?'

Suddenly it seemed to me that he was alert. I had been lulled, in a way, by our literary talk, into thinking of him simply as a pleasant party acquaintance, but all at once I was aware of him as a powerful presence, as he had appeared to me when I first saw him.

'And what,' he asked, 'made you feel this?

Was it something you discovered in her papers?'

'No,' I said, reluctant to speak of Beth's secret life to this stranger. Though suddenly there swept over me, like a wave, the memory of Beth's unfinished novel and I felt a genuine shiver of fear as I looked into the eyes of the man who might very well have been its hero. 'No,' I repeated a little unsteadily, 'nothing specific, just little things–'

The intensity of his gaze, which had been fixed on me, lightened.

'Yes, indeed,' he said lightly, 'how well *do* we know each other, even the most devoted of friends or family?'

'Perhaps,' I said, 'I will simply try to make an evaluation of her work – referring to her life only as it was connected with her work.'

'That would be an excellent idea.'

'Actually,' I said, 'a young American girl, who was working on the papers in the Senate House Library in London, was going to do just that, but I'm afraid it won't be possible now.'

'Not possible?'

Was there just a hint of something other than polite interest in his eyes? I couldn't decide.

'Yes, poor Phoebe. She was killed. Run over and killed.'

'Really. That is very sad. And young, you say? Quite tragic. The road accidents are terrible. Here in Athens they are quite formidable.'

His tone was now conversational again and we talked a little of England and of Athens and other neutral topics.

'It has been a great pleasure to meet you,' he said. 'I wish my wife had been able to be here, but she is at present in our villa in the Mani. I shall look forward to our meeting next spring.'

He bowed again and moved away. 'Ion, my dear fellow,' I heard him say to one of the young men, 'do, please, tell your mother how much Ariadne and I enjoyed the concert.'

I watched his progress through the room. Progress really was an apt word for it, since there was something decidedly regal about him.

'You see,' Cyril was at my elbow, 'he is charming, is he not?'

'Oh yes,' I said, 'very charming.'

I suddenly felt very tired. I looked at my watch and was surprised to see that it was well past midnight. I made my way across the room to where Arnold, still apparently fresh and full of vitality, was holding court.

'Arnold, it's been wonderful, but I'm out of practice with late nights, so I'll say goodnight now.'

'Must you go? Very well, then, Alex will see you back to your hotel. It was so very good of you to come. I do appreciate it, it wouldn't have been the same without you, especially now—'

'I've loved every minute of it,' I said and hugged him.

'Come again soon,' he said. 'Now that I'm seventy I shall begin to count the years left!'

I was glad to be out in the cool night air, walking back with Alex.

'Thank you for coming, Sheila,' he said. 'He was very sad after Beth died. This has helped.'

'Alex,' I said. 'How well did Beth know Theo Andros?'

He turned towards me and in the dark I felt, rather than saw, his surprise. 'How well? Not well, I think. She met him several times at the apartment and they talked a little of literature – Theo is very interested in literature, you understand – and they may have met at parties, you know, circles are quite small in Athens, you meet the same people... Why do you ask?'

'Oh, nothing,' I said, 'just something he said. He seems very keen on her books.'

'Oh well, yes. He too was very sad when he heard of her death. Now I will fetch you tomorrow afternoon and take you to the airport. Your flight is at four-thirty, you said?'

'Oh, Alex, that *is* kind. I can never seem to

get a taxi in Athens.'

'You know what they say?' Alex said. 'To get a taxi in Athens you have to be born in one!'

The following morning I didn't go down to the Plaka and the Parthenon, but turned the other way, up the hill towards the little monastery of Lycabettus. I climbed the steep steps to the small funicular railway and, getting off, walked gratefully in the peace and quiet of the courtyard, where a thin black and white cat lay stretched out in the sun beside one of the great stone jars full of geraniums. I went on into the cool darkness of the monastery, where an old woman sold me a silver crucifix on a chain and a box of Turkish Delight (though one mustn't call it that in Greece) which Hilda is so fond of.

Coming out of the monastery, I walked along to the little café just outside its gates. Here I ordered a salad and a cup of coffee and sat on the terrace, looking down on the city spread out below me. Although I knew that the haze that lay over everything was simply the effect of pollution, it did, somehow, give the view an enchanted quality, a kind of unreality, so that I felt that I was looking down at another world, at another time.

Turning away from the magic before me, I concentrated on my salade niçoise and also on my encounter with Theodore Andros. Last night I had been so overwhelmed by the strength of his personality, his charisma, that I hadn't been able to think rationally. *Was* he the hero of Beth's strange novel? Was he, in fact, the man with whom she had been having an affair? I tried to remember what I had heard about Andros and what I had read in the papers. Certainly never any scandal. He lived with his wife and two daughters in Cephissia, a fashionable area just outside Athens and, apparently, he also had a villa in the remote region of the Mani, where his privacy would be respected. He was a noted philanthropist and had set up several charities as well as making generous contributions to the arts. As I had seen for myself, he had great charm and what appeared to be a sincere wish (always so seductive) to listen to what one had to say, so that one could quite forget his immense wealth and power and regard him simply as a cultivated and agreeable human being. Was this what had appealed to Beth? Certainly, I could see that if one were in his company for any length of time it might be quite easy to fall in love with him.

He provided one more strand in the tangled skein that was Beth's death and Phoebe's murder. But what, if any, part he had played in it I was unable to decide. With a final affectionate glance at the violet-crowned city below me, I got up and made my way slowly down the hill.

Chapter Twelve

'So you see,' I said to Hilda, when I got back, 'I'm more muddled than ever.'

Hilda, who was brushing flea powder into Tolly's coat, looked up at me but made no comment.

'I mean, this Andros man fits so perfectly. He's *exactly* like the hero of that book – well, apart from the spectacles – and I do see that Beth might have been in love with him, even had an affair with him. And, you see, with his reputation to preserve, he couldn't risk anything coming out. So if Phoebe had found out something from Beth's papers, I suppose she might have tried to blackmail him. But how?'

'I expect Mr Andros's business interests bring him to England sometimes,' Hilda said. 'And, since he is an international figure, his arrival would have been mentioned in the press, perhaps even where he was staying, so that it might not have been too difficult for Phoebe to get in touch with him. However, he would not, I imagine, have been a man to give in to blackmail, so I do not doubt, since he is a very rich man, he would have found someone to dispose of Phoebe for him.'

'Oh, really, Hilda!' I exclaimed. 'That's a bit melodramatic!'

'I am merely extending your proposition to its logical conclusion. I do not say that that is what I believe happened. As you say, it *is* overly dramatic and, I would think, unlikely.'

'No, I know he's a very powerful man and he wouldn't want any hint of an affair to be made public, but – no, I can't see him arranging something like that in cold blood! I mean, he likes Jane Austen!'

Hilda regarded me quizzically. 'I cannot imagine how you have managed to survive for so long with such childlike innocence intact,' she said.

'Well, you know what I mean! Still,' I said, 'the fact remains that Phoebe *was* murdered and the only possible motive that I can think of is that her death is in some way connected with Beth.'

'That would seem to be the obvious conclusion.'

Tolly, his patience at an end, gave a great shake, scattering a cloud of flea powder all over Hilda, jumped down off her lap and stalked off out of the room.

'But then, of course, there is the novel,' I said. 'You haven't read it, Hilda, but, honestly, the hero is so like Andros!'

'It is, however, a work of fiction,' Hilda said, 'and I believe it is quite common for writers to combine the characteristics – physical, emotional and social – of several different people in one character. So Beth may have simply given the hero of this book the physical attributes and the powerful position of Mr Andros, but she may well have had some other person in mind.'

'That's true,' I agreed. 'I suppose I might have been jumping to the wrong conclusion.'

'And, of course,' Hilda said, 'there *is* also the possibility that Phoebe's murder had nothing to do with Beth.'

'But—'

'We have only her brother's word that she had no enemies over here. For that matter he may have murdered her himself.'

'But he only came to England after she was dead!'

'There are several flights back and forth across the Atlantic every day. He could easily have been over here before.'

'Why should he want to murder his sister?'

'Money? There may be some sort of problem with a will or a trust – who knows? I am merely pointing out that there are many different aspects to this affair and it seems to me that you would be far better off leaving the whole thing to the police and simply doing what you can to sort out Beth's *literary* problems.'

'Yes,' I said. 'You are absolutely right. I'll see the volume of short stories through the press and find someone suitable to do a critical study of her work and leave it at that.'

'Well, thank goodness that's settled.' Hilda got up and brushed the remaining powder off her skirt. 'I really don't think I can be doing with this stuff any more,' she said. 'What was the name of that anti-flea liquid you get from your vet?'

Following my new resolution, next day I decided to take the morning off and visit Leighton House. It's one of my favourite places and going there is something I always try to do when I'm staying with Hilda. I spent a happy hour wandering round the Arab hall with its discreetly tinkling fountain, admiring the William De Morgan tiles and finally wallowing in the pleasure of the massive canvases, the fine portraits and those classical groups that are, to me, the apotheosis of high Victorian art.

Coming out into the sunshine, I decided to walk through Holland Park and indulge in a little shopping in Kensington High Street. I turned up Melbury Road, passing the rather bleak house where Holman Hunt had lived and Luke Fildes's Tower House, which Edward VII once called the most beautiful house in London. I've always loved walking round here, where so little has changed and on this fine summer morning I seemed to see every leaf and flower fresh and new just as the Pre-Raphaelites who lived here had done. In the park the camellias were long since over round the Orangery, but the beds were full of flowers and the lilies were blooming in the water garden. The peacocks still strutted along the paths of the shrubbery, the colourful 'eyes' in their outspread tails echoing the Pre-Raphaelite theme. I walked up past the remains of old Holland House, now in its new incarnation as an open-air theatre, and on into the Broad Walk leading down to the High Street. By now I was feeling a little tired, so I sat down on one of the benches and watched the passers-by. As I was wondering idly whether the ghost of the Grey Lady that once haunted this spot when it was private and remote, had become discouraged by the noise and traffic and taken herself off to somewhere more peaceful, I became aware that someone had stopped beside me. It was Fiona Packard.

'It *is* Mrs Malory?' she said tentatively.

'Yes, that's right.'

'Do you mind if I join you for a moment?'

'No, of course, please do.'

She looked rather doubtfully at the bench and dusted it lightly with her hand before sitting down. 'I saw you sitting here and I felt I must have a word with you, to explain.'

'Explain?'

'What happened when you came to see Mark.'

'Oh, yes, I see.'

She took a handkerchief from her bag and wiped the dust from the bench off her fingers.

'You must have thought it all very odd,' she said.

'Well, yes, I must say that I did.'

'I don't know what you heard about Mark coming to live with me.'

'Beth seemed to think–'

'That we were lovers? That he was my toy-boy?' She brought the phrase out with some effort and much scorn.

'Well, yes. She was rather upset.'

'Mark was very distressed about that, but he couldn't tell her the truth.'

I looked at her curiously. 'What was the truth?'

She snapped the fastening of her bag shut and laid it on her lap. 'Mark was – is – a very talented young man. I had worked with him on several programmes and admired him greatly. Not just what he was doing but what I felt he was capable of. He had a great future before him. Unfortunately, like some other creative people, living at a very high pitch, trying to do too many things at once, he began to need something to get him through, as he put it. That was when he started taking cocaine. That gave him a greater creative buzz and he took on new projects and so he needed more of the drugs and then more and so it went on until he was in a pretty bad state.'

She paused for a moment, I suppose to let me take in what she had been saying, then she went on. 'As his state got worse, when his dependency was becoming obvious, he got frightened. He adored his mother and he couldn't bear her to know what he had become. He knew he had to move out before she realized what was happening. He asked my advice and I invited him to move in with me.' She looked at me and smiled. 'I suppose it was inevitable that people would jump to the wrong conclusion.'

'I think,' I said cautiously, 'that people couldn't think of any other reason.'

'You mean no one could imagine that I would be capable of an altruistic act? Well, that's fair enough. I've been very successful in my field and I've made a lot of enemies on the way. I've gained a reputation for being hard and ruthless, and I am as far as my work is concerned, but that doesn't mean I have no feelings.'

'Why did you do it, then?' I asked. 'I mean, if you knew what people would say.'

'I've never cared what people might say, so that didn't worry me. I took Mark in and I've been looking after him because I believe in him as a person and as a very rare talent.' She smiled again. 'I'm a very practical person. I can't bear waste, especially the waste of a human being.'

'But surely,' I said, 'it would have been better – easier, anyway – if he'd gone on some rehabilitation scheme?'

'He wouldn't do that. No, I was his only way out.'

'What about your son?' I asked. 'I imagine he was the young man I saw–'

'Giles? He barely took it in. No, Giles lives in his own little world. He's a scientist and one day he's going to win the Nobel Prize for physics. Nothing outside his work has much reality for him. I've never been important in his life – he takes after his father, I suppose. *He* took off for Africa ten years ago to devote his life to some obscure water-borne microbe in the Zambezi!'

'I see.'

'Perhaps *because* Giles has never needed me to do more than provide a roof and some food at the appropriate times I took Mark in. Frustrated maternal instinct, do you think?'

'It was a very noble thing to do,' I said. 'I couldn't have done it.'

She shrugged. 'Nothing noble,' she said. 'I did it because I wanted to. It hasn't been easy, but I think we're getting there.' She looked at my doubtful expression. 'You're thinking of how he was when you saw him?'

'Well, yes.'

'He's been very much worse than that! But actually we have had a few setbacks. His mother's death, of course. He'd been much improved until then. He'd spoken to her on the telephone. I believe he might even have been able to go and see her – but then–'

'I can imagine.'

'He went right back for a bit and it's been a long haul since then.'

'I wonder–' I paused. 'I wonder, has his father telephoned recently?'

'Ah, yes. Fortunately I answered the phone and was able to take a message.'

'You know about his father's marriage, then?'

'Yes.'

'And about the baby?'

'The baby?'

'John is marrying shortly,' I said, 'because a baby is due in about six weeks.'

'I see,' she said. 'Well, I certainly won't tell Mark *that*. In fact I don't propose to tell him about any of it. I see no point in unsettling him unnecessarily.'

'Helen might ring,' I said. 'She is going to be very distressed about it all – she adores her father – and she might want to talk to Mark about it.'

'I'll cross that bridge when I come to it.

Though I don't think Helen will ring. She doesn't approve of me.'

'Miss Packard,' I said, 'something rather disturbing has happened that I think you ought to know about.' And I told her about Phoebe's murder and all the attendant circumstances.

'I see,' she said thoughtfully. 'I imagine what you want to ask me is, do I think that Mark had anything to do with this girl's death?'

'Well, yes, I suppose I do.'

'I have never heard of this Phoebe Walters and I am quite sure Mark hasn't. Furthermore, he hardly ever goes out and certainly not on his own. Part of his condition is that he cannot face the outside world. He will only go out with me. Does that answer your question?'

'Yes, it does. Thank you. I didn't really imagine ... but I'm glad to know Mark could have had nothing to do with the affair.'

She looked at me quizzically. 'You are, in a manner of speaking, investigating it?'

'No, nothing like that,' I said. 'It's just that, as Beth's literary executor, I'm involved. And she was my friend. I want very much to have the whole thing cleared up.'

'Mark said something about a biography.'

'I was going to write one, but not now. There'll just be a scholarly volume of literary criticism if I can find someone suitable to do it.'

'Mark will be relieved. I think he found the idea of someone ferreting about in his mother's life rather distasteful.'

'Yes, I understand. Do you think he will be able to get back to normal – how he was before – and able to work again?'

'Yes, I'm sure he will. We talk a lot about various projects and he is getting really interested again. I hope it won't be too long before he's fit to get back again.'

Her voice was animated. Impulsively I put my hand on her arm and said, 'What you are doing is really marvellous!'

She gave me one of her rare smiles. 'We only do what we want to do, that's what my mother used to say, and I believe it's true.'

'It really was quite extraordinary,' I said to Hilda when I told her what had happened. 'She is a remarkable woman.'

'A very sensible one, certainly,' Hilda said approvingly. 'She does what she sees to be right, unhampered by any consideration of the outside world. I admire that.'

'Oh so do I,' I agreed. 'It's just that, well, there don't seem to be any *feelings–*'

'And none the worse for that,' Hilda said. 'Too many feelings only obscure the issue.'

'I suppose you're right, but I would have thought that Mark needed a great deal of love, especially after losing Beth so suddenly.'

'Love can come later. What is needed now is practical help and it seems to me that this Packard person is going the right way about it.'

'Well, anyway,' I said, 'I think we can say that Mark wasn't involved with Phoebe's death.'

Hilda folded her table napkin and placed it neatly in its silver ring. 'I'll bring the coffee into the sitting-room, shall I?' she said. 'You go on through.'

I must say it's always nice at Hilda's to sit down properly to meals in the dining-room rather than slothing in front of the television with a tray as Michael and I usually do. Not that I'd want to do it always (I've grown lazy), but for a little while it's pleasant to resume the more civilized ways of my youth.

'There we are.' Hilda laid down the tray and Tolly, who had followed her into the room, promptly leapt on to the coffee table and put his head into the milk jug to investigate its contents. '*No*, Tolly!' Hilda said firmly but ineffectually. I leaned forward and picked up the miscreant. He eyed me blandly, then, giving me a perfunctory bite on the wrist, he jumped down and went over to the windowseat, where he sat looking enigmatic, like some presiding deity of the house.

'So who does that leave us with?' I asked,

as Hilda poured the coffee. 'There's John and perhaps this man Andros–'

'There is one other person you don't seem to have thought of.'

'Who's that?'

'Your friend Bill North.'

'Bill?'

'Why not? He might have been having an affair with Beth.'

'Oh, I don't think that's very likely. I mean, they did have a little thing together at Oxford, but that's years ago and then Beth married John and, much later, Bill married Anne – who's young and really quite attractive – and they've just been friends ever since. I can't see anything *rekindling* between them after all these years!'

'But if there *was* something – not necessarily an affair – perhaps something Beth knew about Bill North that she wrote down, something that Phoebe might have found among her papers, something she might blackmail him with. That might be a possible motive. As a Cabinet Minister, he's very susceptible to anything that might be considered scandalous by the media.'

'You're right,' I said. 'I'm sure there wasn't an affair, but they were good friends and it's quite possible Bill might have confided in Beth if he was in trouble of any kind. Still,' I continued doubtfully, 'I can't imagine Bill actually *killing* anyone.'

'I don't suppose anyone can imagine any of their friends killing anyone,' Hilda observed, 'but it happens nevertheless.'

'One thing,' I said, 'since Parliament is sitting it shouldn't be difficult to find out where he was that day. I must try and get hold of a copy of Hansard. Do you think they have it at Kensington Library? I'll go along there tomorrow.'

I was able to check Hansard for the day Phoebe was killed and found, to my relief, that Bill had made a ministerial statement to the House in the afternoon and had been involved in an early evening debate later on.

'So that's all right,' I said. 'Not that I thought for a moment that he could have,

but it's good to be able to eliminate someone else.'

'Anyway,' Hilda said, 'I thought you were
going to leave it all to the police.'

'You're right,' I said. 'I intend to turn my
back on the whole affair and absolutely
nothing will make me change my mind this
time.'

Which is always a silly thing to say.

Chapter Thirteen

'Goodness,' I said, laying down the letter I had just received, 'I never knew that Beth was published in Poland!'

'Really?' Hilda looked up from her own correspondence.

'Yes, I've just had this letter from a man in Warsaw, saying that he's planning a review article about one of her books that's been translated into Polish.'

'Well, that is very satisfactory.'

I looked over the letter again. 'Apparently it's quite a recent thing, sometime this year, I gather. I wonder why Ralph didn't say anything about it.'

'Is it relevant?'

'Perhaps not – but I knew about the French and German editions and the Dutch and Italian and there's the American ones, of course. I feel I *ought* to know, somehow. I think I'll phone John. I've been meaning to talk to him anyway, to see how Helen took his news.'

It took me quite a while to get hold of John, but eventually I managed to get him on his mobile. But he didn't seem to know anything about a Polish edition of Beth's work.

'Ralph would be the person to ask,' he said. 'He'd know.'

'Yes, I suppose so, but I'm afraid if I get in touch with him he'll badger me about this Life of Beth he wants me to write!'

'You're definitely not going to do it then?' John asked.

'No, I really couldn't. Not now.'

'Yes, I see.' There was a pause, then he said, 'I'm sorry, Sheila. I expect I've messed things up for you rather.'

'No,' I said, 'it's not just that. It's all become so difficult. I wrote to you about this girl Phoebe being killed. You got my letter?'

'Yes, yes I did. Actually, I've been meaning to get back to you about it ... I had a call from the police, as well. Because of the connection with Beth, I suppose. Though I hadn't had much to do with this Phoebe person. I did have a letter from her saying that she wanted to talk to me about Beth for the thing she was writing, and then she came up and spoke to me at the memorial service. But that's all. Do you know, the police wanted to know where I was on the day she died – wasn't that extraordinary, as if *I* had something to do with it! Why should I want to kill a girl I hardly know?'

'They seem to think she was blackmailing someone,' I said. 'She might have come across something in Beth's papers–'

'Good God! What an extraordinary thing! Something about me and Sally, you mean? But Beth's dead – who would she want to tell? I mean what else would she be blackmailing me about?'

'I really don't know, John. Were the police satisfied about your alibi?'

'Alibi? Oh, yes. I was having meetings all day – bankers and money people, every minute accounted for. But still, it was an unpleasant experience, being suspected like that.'

'Yes, it must have been.'

'And you think the police believe that she was killed because of something to do with Beth?'

'It seems the only possible motive.' There was a brief silence and then I asked, 'How is Helen? Did you go down and see her?'

John hesitated for a moment. 'Well, actually, I haven't been able to get down there,' he said. 'It's been pretty hectic here – the financial situation and so forth. I wrote her a letter explaining it all.'

'I see.'

'I hope to be able to get down there next week,' John said hastily. 'Certainly before the wedding.'

I didn't reply and he continued, 'It really has been a difficult time, Sheila. I'm sure you understand.'

'Yes. Yes, of course.'

There was a crackle on the line and John said, 'I'm afraid it's breaking up – these wretched mobiles! I'll ring you soon.'

There was a further crackle and then silence.

I decided to try and speak to Ralph Hastings's assistant – Selina, no, Samantha, that was it – rather than Ralph himself, so I rang the office early on the assumption that he wouldn't be in until the streets were aired, as my father used to say. I was right.

'Oh, Mrs Malory, I'm so sorry, he isn't in yet. Can I take a message?'

'I expect *you* can help me, actually,' I said. 'It's about Beth Blackmore's foreign rights. I was wondering if there were any more East European translations, beside the Polish one?'

'Oh, I'm sorry. I can't help you there. Mr Hastings does all the foreign things himself.'

'Perhaps you could just have a look in the files for me?'

'Yes, of course. Would you mind hanging on for a minute?'

She was back quite quickly. 'I'm so sorry, but all the foreign rights things are in the filing cabinet in Mr Hastings's office and I'm afraid I can't get at them because it's locked.'

'Oh, I see.'

'I'll tell Mr Hastings you were enquiring about them,' Samantha said, 'and he'll get back to you.'

'No,' I said hastily, 'never mind, it wasn't important. I'll ring him some other time.'

I thought it was a little odd that no one in the office knew about these things, but since Ralph's publishing house was very much a one-man band I suppose he liked to keep a personal eye on things. I decided, reluctantly, that I'd have to have a word with him about it before I replied to the man in Warsaw.

I telephoned Nicola that evening to see if there was any more news.

'No, nothing. That CID Sergeant has been round here a couple of times, to have another look at her room and to have another word with Ben, but it doesn't seem to have led them anywhere.'

'They got in touch with Beth's husband, John Blackmore,' I said, 'but that didn't lead anywhere, either.'

'Actually, I told Sergeant Mortimer about the stolen carbon and he said he'd like to speak to you, so I gave him your address and telephone number. Was that all right?'

'Yes, of course. But as we've all agonized over *that* with no result, I don't think I can add anything useful. How about Ben, by the way? Is he still in England?'

'Yes. He goes back next week. They've adjourned the inquest, but they released the body so Phoebe's to be cremated tomorrow. He'll be flying back next Wednesday.'

'You'll miss him,' I said casually.

Nicola laughed. 'Well, as a matter of fact, I'm going over to Philadelphia next month. I hadn't fixed up anything about my holiday this year and, well, I've always wanted to see the States and Ben was kind enough to invite me–'

'He's nice, isn't he? At least, I only saw him very briefly, but he seemed very pleasant.'

Sergeant Mortimer turned up on the doorstep the next day. He was a neat-looking, compact man with thinning brown hair and tired grey eyes.

'Sorry to bother you, Mrs Malory, but we have to follow up everything, and in this case there's little enough to go on.'

'Yes, I quite understand. Do please come in. Can I get you a cup of tea or coffee?'

'No, I'm fine, thanks.' He sat down rather gingerly on one of Hilda's small Victorian chairs and produced a notebook. 'Now, Miss Fairbairn says that Phoebe Walters stole something from some library, is that right?'

I told him about Phoebe working on Beth's papers in the Senate House Library and how it appeared that she had stolen the missing carbon.

'And would this paper have any special value, would you say?' he asked.

'Not any monetary value, no. And, quite honestly, I wouldn't say value of any kind. The only thing is that the pages of the carbon had been stapled together and those of the original had not.'

'And what would you say was the significance of that?'

'Well, all I can think of is that there was something else attached to the carbon, something that had got stapled to it by mistake.'

'What sort of thing?'

'I don't know.'

'Some other document, you think? Something that might be of importance to someone? Something that Phoebe Walters might be able to turn to her own advantage?'

'Yes.'

'Blackmail, in fact?'

'The thought had crossed my mind.'

Sergeant Mortimer settled himself more comfortably in his chair and regarded me in silence for a moment. Then he said, 'Mrs Malory, can you think of anyone she might have been blackmailing?'

I shook my head. 'I have thought about it quite a bit, actually. But I really can't think of anyone—'

'You were a close friend of Beth Blackmore. Do you know of anything in her personal life that might have made someone else a subject for blackmail?'

'No,' I said, perhaps too quickly, because he looked at me sharply.

'You do realize that this is a murder inquiry, a very serious affair, so we need every scrap of information we can get.'

'Yes, of course,' I said, 'and I wish I could be more helpful, but really there is nothing I can tell you.'

'Right, well, if you do think of anything, Mrs Malory, perhaps you would give me a ring.' He felt in his pocket and produced a card. 'This is the number.'

'Thank you, yes, I will.'

'One final thing. Could you tell me where you were on the day that Phoebe Walters was killed?'

Like John, I was rather taken aback at being asked this question. My surprise must have shown in my face since he said with a slight smile, 'Just for the record, of course.'

'Of course,' I echoed. 'Let me see, it was the twenty-seventh, wasn't it?'

'Yes, that's right.'

I opened my handbag and got out my diary. 'The twenty-seventh ... yes, here it is. I was at the Senate House Library for most of the day working on Beth's papers – I did nip out for a quick pub lunch, just around the corner – and I left at about four-thirty. It was just the beginning of the rush hour so I didn't get back here until, oh, I suppose, six o'clock. Then I spent the rest of the evening at home with my cousin.'

'Thank you very much, Mrs Malory.' He flipped his notebook shut and stood up.

'And don't forget anything at all you can think of–'

When he had gone, I said to Hilda, 'I did feel awful not telling him about things, but honestly, I don't think anything I might have said would be any help. I mean, we've been over it all again and again.'

'It is never comfortable to tell a lie,' Hilda said.

'I don't think I *lied*, exactly. I was just a bit economical with the truth.'

Hilda smiled wryly. 'That really is one of the most useful phrases to be coined this century.'

'Well, you see,' I felt, somehow, that I had to justify my silence, 'you see, he doesn't know any of the people involved and he could very easily put two and two together and come up with quite the wrong answer. Things really *aren't* black and white, are they, especially in this particular situation.'

'No, you're probably right,' Hilda said, 'it would be very easy to oversimplify things.

Of course,' she went on, 'it may just be that *you* still feel you can solve the thing yourself and you don't want him butting in!'

I was just about to embark on a vigorous denial of this, when there was a heavy thump and a furious face appeared at the window.

'Oh, *look* at him,' Hilda cried. 'He's absolutely *soaked!* He would go out in the rain–'

She went out of the room and reappeared with a struggling Tolly wrapped in a towel.

'Now do stay still while I try and get you dry!' Tolly broke free and leapt up on to the sofa, where he left a large damp patch, and engaged in an elaborate toilet, with much licking of paws and cries of dissatisfaction at the nature of the weather that were only quelled when Hilda brought him a saucer of newly cooked fish, which he ate with some satisfaction, scattering the pieces over the sofa cushions in his enthusiasm.

I was still brooding over Hilda's accusation later that evening when the telephone rang. It was John Blackmore. His voice was very shaky and I could hardly hear what he was saying.

'Sheila, something dreadful's happened!'

'John, what is it?'

'Oh God, it's terrible – I can't believe–' He broke off.

'John, what *is* it?'

'It's Helen, she's – she's tried to kill herself!'

Chapter Fourteen

I sat down on the hall seat and held the telephone closer to my ear.

'Is she all right?' I asked.

'Yes, thank God. They found her in time.' His voice was husky, as if he had been crying.

'When did it happen?'

'Yesterday. Well, they found her yesterday morning, she had taken some stuff the night before–'

'Have you seen her?'

'No,' he was sobbing now. 'No – she won't see me.'

'Oh, John, I'm so sorry.'

There was a moment's pause while he pulled himself together and then he said, 'Sheila, could you go? I've got to know how she is.'

'Where is she? Still in hospital?'

'No, the doctor said she could go back to college after they'd – they'd seen to her.'

'I see.'

'Sheila, I know it's a great deal to ask, but I'm absolutely desperate. I know it's all my fault, and I can't do anything... Please!'

'Yes,' I said. 'All right, I'll go.'

'She's in the college sanatorium, they're keeping an eye on her there. You'll need to see her tutor first, a Miss Macdonald. Sheila, I'm *so* grateful. I can't begin to tell you.'

'Yes, well, I'll go tomorrow, first thing. So if you could let this Miss Macdonald know that I'm coming.'

Hilda was deeply shocked when I told her what had happened.

'That wretched man!' she exclaimed. 'What did he expect when he didn't tell her face to face, fobbing her off with a letter like that!'

'Yes, I'm afraid John isn't the most

sensitive of people. Perhaps you get like that if you're successful in business. I may have to stay overnight so I'll just go and pack a case and see if I can book a room at the Garden House.'

This time I didn't idle about in Cambridge, but took a taxi straight to Newnham. Miss Macdonald turned out to be a tall, auburn-haired woman in her early fifties – a bit like Beth, to look at – with an attractive Scottish accent.

'Helen is very much better now,' she said. 'She was very disturbed when she heard that her father wanted to visit her.'

'Well,' I said, 'since it was her father's behaviour that drove her to do it, I suppose that's not surprising.'

'Really? She hasn't said anything and, naturally, we haven't pressed her.'

I explained about Beth and Helen's reaction to her mother's affair and then about John's marriage and the baby that was due very soon now.

Miss Macdonald sighed. 'I see,' she said.

'It doesn't excuse what Helen has done, but it certainly explains it. Poor girl.'

'Does she know that I've come to see her?'

'Yes, she seems quite happy about that.' She got up. 'I'll take you along to the sanatorium.'

I followed her along the quiet, white-painted corridors and she opened a door into a large room with several beds in it. Helen was the only person there. She was leafing through a book and looked up as the door opened.

'Here's Mrs Malory, Helen,' Miss Macdonald said. She smiled at me. 'I'll leave you to have a chat. Please come and have a word with me on your way out.'

I drew up a chair and sat by Helen's bed. Her face was pale and her hair was straight and lank. She looked thoroughly wretched. I took her hand in mine.

'Helen, my dear girl, I'm so glad you're all right.'

She shrugged and withdrew her hand from mine. 'You haven't asked me why I did it, but then I expect you know. You know all about him and that Sally girl, about the baby and all the awfulness.'

'Well–'

'I expect everyone knew.'

'No, I'm sure–'

'Do you think Mother knew? It must have been going on a long time if there's a baby. Do you think that's *why* she had an affair herself – to pay him out?'

'Helen, I don't know, I really don't know.'

'I hated her, and now I hate him as well. There's no one left–'

Suddenly she began to cry, great racking sobs. I held her close, thankful that she was able to give way at last, knowing that it was the best thing for her.

When she was a little calmer I said, 'Helen, you must try and put all this behind you. You're young, you have all your life in front of you. I know it's difficult to believe, but you will get over this, you will be able to live your own life. You must promise me you'll never do anything like that again.'

She reached under her pillow for a tissue and wiped her eyes. 'I wanted to punish him,' she said, 'and that girl. I hated them so much!'

'Hate will only destroy you. You know that in your heart, now, don't you?'

She nodded. 'Yes, you're right. But if the hate goes, there will be nothing. I will be so lonely.'

'You must think about yourself now, not about anyone else. You must rebuild your own life. That's what Mark is trying to do.'

'Mark? What do you mean?'

I told her about Mark and Fiona Packard. She listened in silence and then she said, 'I never knew. I just thought it was, you know, the Packard woman cradle-snatching. I never dreamt... Poor Mark.' She shook her head sadly. 'We're both pretty hopeless wrecks!'

'No,' I said vehemently, 'you're not, neither of you. You've both got the opportunity to rebuild your lives. You can both achieve so much. What about your degree?

Did you finish your exams?'

'No – I don't know what will happen. I suppose they'll give me an aegrotat. It doesn't matter. I don't see myself doing anything academic.'

'What do you *want* to do?'

She shrugged. 'I don't know. At least, there was something, but I thought Father wouldn't want me to ... not that *that* matters now!'

'What was it?'

'There's this education project out in Kenya, teaching in backward village communities. The college has some sort of connection with it and one of the women teachers was over here last term to talk about it–'

'It sounds like a good thing,' I said. 'I'm sure it's worth thinking about.' I got up. 'I'm going now, and you must have a rest, I'm sure you're still very weak. I'm staying overnight in Cambridge so I'll be in to see you tomorrow.'

Miss Macdonald's room was flooded with

sunshine and the French doors leading out into the garden were wide open. The irises were over, but the herbaceous borders were bright with colour.

'How did you find her?' she asked.

'Still very unhappy,' I said, 'but I think the worst is over now. I will tell her father that she'll be better left to herself for a while. Actually, she ought to get right away. She was saying something about this teaching project in Kenya.'

'Oh yes, the Sidgwick Memorial Trust. You think she's interested in that?'

'It's possible. I think it might be just the thing.'

'I'll talk to her about it. She would need to think about it very carefully, it's not the sort of thing to go plunging into without a proper commitment.'

'Yes, I do understand that, but it occurs to me that this might just be the thing that Helen has been looking for for a long time. I'll be in again tomorrow and perhaps you will have spoken to her about it by then.

Thank you for all you have done for her. I do appreciate how difficult something like this is for the college.'

'I'm afraid it is becoming more and more common nowadays,' Miss Macdonald said sadly. 'Young people seem to be under so much stress – work, relationships, general *angst*–'

'Life was so much simpler in my day,' I said. 'Rules were stricter, you knew where you were and what was expected of you. Less freedom, but perhaps that was no bad thing. Nowadays there are no rules and everything seems to be in a state of flux. How can they have any certainty about people or situations? Still, I think Helen will pull through.'

The next day Helen certainly seemed much better. She was dressed and sitting in a chair by the window. She even greeted me with a smile.

'Thank you for coming, Sheila,' she said. 'It's helped me see things in perspective, somehow.'

'I'm glad. Look, Helen, term's nearly over – have you thought what you're going to do? Where you'll go? Only I thought you might like to come and stay with me at Taviscombe for a bit, just until you decide what you want to do.'

'That's very kind of you, but I've arranged to stay with Julia. She's the friend who saw Mother on Hydra–'

'Yes, I remember.'

'I've stayed with her before. Her parents have been very kind.'

'Well, if that's what you want.'

'It's all right, I'm not going to do anything silly. I promise.'

'No, I'm sure you're not.'

Helen moved her chair round a little so that she was facing me directly.

'Actually, I think I wanted someone to find me. I took the tablets late at night, knowing that Rosie would call for me in the morning. She has the room next door and we usually go down to breakfast together.'

'It wasn't very kind of you,' I said, 'to

expose her to that kind of shock.'

'No, it was awful of me, I see that now. It's just that I felt so miserable I wanted everyone to be sorry. It was very stupid and childish of me and I'm really sorry.'

'Well, I can see that it was a horrible situation for you.'

'But that's why I want to do something worthwhile *now*. I've decided I really do want to go to Kenya and work on this project. That's one of the reasons I want to stay with Julia. Her father's a headmaster and I want to see what he thinks about it all.'

'I think that's a splendid idea,' I said. 'A very mature decision.'

Helen smiled sadly. 'I've done quite a bit of growing up in the last few days. Sheila, what should I do about Mark?'

'Write him a letter, let him know what you're doing. Don't mention your father – Fiona doesn't think he's strong enough to take that yet – but just make it a loving letter. And keep in touch. He'll need you

301

when he's back to normal again.'

She nodded. 'Thank you, I'll do that.'

I got up. 'Keep in touch with me, too, won't you?'

She got up and we hugged each other. 'Thank you for everything, Sheila. I'll never forget your kindness.'

When I got back I rang John and told him what had happened.

'Thank God she's all right,' he said. 'What do you think I should do?'

'Leave things. She needs time to get over it. One day she'll get in touch with you.'

'But–'

'It's the best thing you can do for her.'

He sighed. 'You're probably right. What do you think about this African thing? I must say I'm not very happy about that.'

'No, she thought you wouldn't approve, that's why she didn't go for it before. No, I think it's all right. It will do her good to get right away and concentrate on other people's difficulties for a while.'

'I suppose so.'

'Actually, Helen has always seemed to me to be a fundamentally serious girl, certainly a girl with very high principles. I think this is just the thing she's needed all along.'

'Oh dear,' John said wearily, 'my poor children, Mark and now Helen. I've failed them both, haven't I?'

'You weren't the only one,' I said, and I told him about Beth's affair and how badly Helen had taken it.

'So *that's* why she wouldn't have anything to do with her mother!'

'And that's why she saw your marriage and the baby as the final betrayal.'

'Oh God!'

'You never suspected about Beth?' I asked. 'You've no idea who the man could be?'

'No. It never occurred to me... As I said, we weren't that close these last few years. I was away a lot and Beth was often down at the cottage or in Greece. Goodness, Sheila, you've really shaken me over this!'

'I didn't feel I could betray Helen's

confidence before, but now – well, it seemed only right to tell you. I hope all goes well with your marriage to Sally.'

'I must try and do better for this baby than I did before.'

'Yes, I expect you will.'

'It really is an extraordinary feeling,' I said to Hilda as I came back into the sitting-room, 'to see what you think is a perfectly ordinary, stable family, simply falling apart! It's like something out of a Greek tragedy!'

'Hardly as extreme as that,' she remarked. 'Though there have been two deaths and one near death.'

'I still wonder about Beth's accident,' I said.

'Don't,' Hilda said firmly. 'It will do no good.'

'It's all such a jumble – and where does Phoebe fit into it all?'

'Try and put it out of your mind. Would you like the television on? There's quite a good archaeological programme on soon –

something they dug out of a peat bog.'

'No, you watch it. I just want to make another phone call.'

Suddenly I wanted to talk to Bill North. Because of all that had happened about Beth and her family, I had the strange feeling that my memories of the past were being eroded, destroyed even, one by one. It was an unpleasant feeling and I felt the need to talk to someone who shared that past and who might make me feel safe again.

By great good fortune Bill was in and answered the phone himself.

'Bill? It's Sheila. Sorry to bother you like this, but some rather awful things have been happening and I felt I'd like to talk to you. Can you spare a few moments?'

'Oh, Sheila, look, I'm so sorry, but I'm just on my way out. Something I have to go to. But hang on, just a minute while I get my diary open. Yes, that's all right. Can you manage eleven-thirty tomorrow morning, just for an hour? I'm in and out of the House, so it would have to be up in town.

Could you manage that?'

'Yes, that would be fine. Where?'

'How about the buffet in the Sainsbury Wing of the National Gallery?'

'Yes, lovely. I'll see you then.'

'This is rather nice,' I said as we sat by the window looking out over Trafalgar Square.

'Yes, it's my secret retreat, when I want to get away for a little while,' Bill said.

'And I see you're in disguise!' I indicated the rather scruffy leather jacket he was wearing.

'Yes, well, it helps. If you're rather easily recognized (and the television certainly makes that inevitable) it does lay you open to being waylaid by people with problems. It's amazing what a difference wearing just one shabby item of clothing will make.' He laughed. 'People look at you, think they recognize you and then think, no, it couldn't be!'

'The price of fame.'

'Oh, yes. Don't think I'm knocking it. But

just sometimes you just want to be an ordinary person. Now then, what's the matter? You sounded really desolate on the phone.'

'I felt a bit desolate,' I said and I told him about John and Helen and Mark.

'God!' he said. 'What a mess!'

'That's not all,' I said, and I told him about Phoebe's death and the police inquiry.

He shook his head. 'I don't believe it!'

'It's true. It looks as though she'd been blackmailing someone with some document she found among Beth's papers.'

'That's incredible. Come to think of it, though, she did say she was going to get in touch with me to talk about Beth and she never did. I'm afraid I've been so busy these last few weeks I hadn't really thought about that.'

'So you only saw her that once, at the memorial service?'

'Yes, that's right. I must say, she looked like a perfectly ordinary, nice, polite girl. I

wouldn't have put her down as a black-
mailer!'

'No, that's what I felt. But her brother – he
came over here when she was killed – said
she wasn't nice at all.'

'And do the police have any idea who
might have killed her?'

'I don't think so. They've got the van – I
told you about the van, didn't I – but there's
nothing there to help them. There's so little
to go on.'

Bill put some sugar in his coffee and
stirred it, watching the swirls made by the
spoon. 'I still can't get over poor Helen.
She's really all right, you say?'

'Yes. It was really a cry for help, as they
say, that and a wish to hurt her father.'

'God, yes, fancy old John... And a baby,
too.'

'Helen was in a pretty fragile state
anyway,' I said, 'because of her mother.'

'Yes.'

'I suppose Beth's death was the catalyst, if
that's the word I want, that made all these

things happen or at least come out into the open. And I'm still not happy about that.'

'What do you mean?'

'It seems such a *peculiar* way to die, so unnecessary, if you see what I mean, such a stupid accident.'

'But it was an accident.'

'Yes, I know that, but still... Oh, I'm sorry, I'm not making much sense, am I? It's just that things seem to have been falling apart lately and I feel – like I said before – *desolate*! Still it *has* helped to talk to you.'

'I'm glad. Sorry it's been such a brief interlude. We must have lunch together sometime soon.'

'Lovely. Oh, Bill, I knew there was something else I wanted to ask you. Did you know that Beth had sold the rights of her books in Poland? Only I've had a letter from someone in Warsaw who talks about a Polish translation. Beth never told me about it and John doesn't seem to have heard about it, either.'

Bill looked surprised. 'That's odd,' he

said. 'Almost the last time I saw her she was saying that she would have liked some Eastern European translations and wondered what Ralph was doing about it. She said she was going to speak to him about it.'

'Oh, how peculiar. Oh well, there's nothing for it – I'll have to get in touch with Ralph myself and hope he doesn't try to bully me about the Life!'

'He can be very persuasive!'

Bill started to rummage in his pockets for a tip to leave the waitress.

'Do let me,' I said, picking up my handbag.

'No, it's all right, I know I've got something here.' He pulled out a handful of objects from the pocket of his jacket and laid them on the table: car keys, a packet of cigarettes, a disposable lighter and a handful of coins. 'Ah, here we are.' He picked out a pound coin and placed it beside his empty cup. He saw that I was looking at the cigarette packet and laughed. 'You must promise not to tell Anne. I officially gave up when the children wore born but there are times when only a cigarette will do!'

'Oh I know,' I said sympathetically. 'I gave up when Peter had to, to keep him company. But every so often the temptation is very strong!'

'How long will you be in London?' Bill asked.

'Not much longer. I've almost finished what I have to do in the Senate House Library, the rest I can work on at home.'

'Well, before you go, come and have dinner with us. Anne's up north with the children at the moment, but she'll be back soon. I'll give you a ring. Forgive me if I dash now. I've got a Select Committee straight after lunch and my PPS will be furious with me if I don't go through things with him first!'

He gave me a wave and was gone.

I went out more slowly and wandered round the gallery for a while, taking comfort in the beauty and tranquillity of the paintings. I stood for a long time before an

early Italian triptych, enjoying the con-
temporary detail – the rich velvet clothes of
the patron, kneeling smugly, hands
together, in the bottom right-hand corner,
the lively little dog frisking about behind
him, the formalized trees clustered in the
background and the unchanging landscape
under a clear blue Italian sky.

Chapter Fifteen

'I think I must be getting back home soon,' I said to Hilda. 'I've nearly finished all I have to do at the library. Besides, Michael wants to go away for the weekend at the end of the month, so I'll have to be back then to look after the animals. I think you were right about him needing a little time on his own, but I got the sort of feeling when he telephoned the other evening that he's finding it a bit much doing the household chores and looking after the animals as well as being at work all day!'

'Tolly and I will miss you,' Hilda said.

'And I'll miss you, too. It's been lovely being here with you both. And I must say,' I went on, watching Tolly crashing about in the sink in a vain attempt to leap up and bat the kitchen blind cord, 'it's going to seem very dull at home!'

Hilda smiled. 'When you come again,' she said, 'I expect Tolly will have calmed down.'

'Don't you believe it,' I exclaimed. 'Siameses never calm down! They merely graduate to a more refined form of wickedness.'

The telephone rang and Hilda went to answer it. 'It's for you,' she said, coming back into the kitchen. 'That Ralph Hastings man. I said I wasn't sure if you were in–'

'Oh, it's all right. I've got to speak to him sometime.'

'Sheila?' Ralph's voice seemed even more suave than usual. 'Samantha tells me that you telephoned the other day when I was out. Something about foreign rights?'

'Yes, it was about Beth's East European rights.'

'Ah, yes.' There was a moment's silence, then, 'Perhaps you would like to come in to the office and we could go into the matter.'

'Yes, that's fine. Can you manage today? I have to go into the Senate House Library this morning, so if you're free this afternoon?'

'Would three-thirty be suitable?'

'Yes. Splendid. I'll see you then.'

On an impulse, after I had finished looking through the papers I was working on, I opened the file of Beth's contracts. They were neatly put together in chronological order in the file. Beth was a tidy and methodical person and, since she employed no agent ('Ralph and I are old friends, what do I need an agent for?') she looked after her own literary affairs. I found the contracts for the foreign rights – America, France, Italy, Germany, Japan – attached to the main contract for each book, but there was no sign of anything relating to Poland or any other East European country. I was puzzled and got out the correspondence with Ralph. I went through it thoroughly, but still found no sort of reference.

Feeling very mystified, I went into the nearby Pizza Place and ate my way through a rather stodgy margherita, puzzling all the while about what the explanation might be, but I came to no conclusion.

Since there was half an hour before my appointment with Ralph, I walked round Bedford Square, enjoying the afternoon sunshine and the sight of grass and trees, pleasant greenery, albeit rather dusty, in the centre of the city, and realizing that it was not just Michael and the animals that I was missing, but the sea and the moors of Taviscombe as well.

When I got to Ralph's office, a young girl I hadn't seen before met me in Reception and took me through. Samantha wasn't in the outer office and, as he came forward to greet me, Ralph said to the girl, 'Tell the switchboard to hold any calls, please, Janice, I don't want to be disturbed.'

'No Samantha today?' I said chattily.

He looked a little confused. 'No, she's on holiday.'

In fact, Ralph looked more ill at ease than I had ever seen him.

'Now,' he said, 'what can I do for you?

Something to do with foreign rights?'

'Yes. I had a letter from someone in Warsaw who wants to write a review article about one of Beth's books that's been translated into Polish. I hadn't realized that any of them had been.'

'Yes, well, it's fairly recent.'

'John hadn't heard about it and Bill North said that the last time he saw Beth she said she was going to ask you about the possibility of East European rights.'

Ralph was silent, fiddling with a heavy brass paperknife on his desk.

'But,' I went on, 'if any of the books have already been published in translation in Poland, then the negotiations must have been made, and the contracts signed, long before Beth died. I mean, books don't just *appear*, it all takes quite a while.'

'Yes, of course.'

'And,' I continued, 'I checked Beth's files today – the files where she kept all her contracts – and there are no contracts for Polish translations.'

Ralph laid down the paperknife and aligned it with concentrated care with the edge of his blotter.

'I see I shall have to explain to you exactly what has happened.'

'Yes,' I said. 'I think you must.'

He leaned back in his chair in an unsuccessful effort to look at ease. 'You may or may not know that this publishing house has on occasion gone through very difficult times.'

'I had heard something of the kind, yes.'

'It has always been a question of liquidity. In fact, things once got to such a state that a relatively small sum stood between being able to continue or having to sell up. A very large conglomerate was anxious to take us over. We have several prestigious authors as well as Beth and our list would be well worth having.' He placed his hands on the desk and leaned forward. 'This publishing house is my life. I care for it more than anything in the world. It's dominated my life, destroyed my marriage, even, but it means everything to me. I couldn't bear to think of it being swallowed up in some great faceless organization, losing its identity. Can you understand that?'

'Yes. Yes, I can.'

'Then perhaps you may understand why I yielded to temptation. Offers were made for translation rights in Poland, Czechoslavakia, and Hungary – for all Beth's books. It wasn't an immense amount of money, but quite a considerable sum nevertheless. It added up to enough to get the firm out of its difficulties. I didn't want to hold things up... The temptation was too strong. I forged Beth's name on the contracts and I didn't tell her about the deals. I never intended to keep the money for ever. I knew that there would be a fairly substantial sum coming in later in the year from some film and television rights. I thought of it as a sort of bridging loan, I suppose. I was always going to give Beth the money.' He looked at me earnestly. 'You do believe me, don't you?'

I shrugged. 'Yes, I think I do.'

'But then Beth died and so I thought I'd hang on for a bit longer and time went on–'

'So Beth's novels have been translated into Czech and Hungarian as well?'

'Yes, some of them.'

I was silent for a moment and then I said, 'Did you know that Phoebe Walters was killed?'

'Phoebe–?' He looked at me in bewilderment. 'Oh, that girl, yes, I had heard. The police got on to me. Apparently they came across some correspondence we had. Wanted to know if I had seen her. But what on earth has that got to do with all this?'

'And had you seen her?'

'No. Well, just that time at Beth's memorial service. She said she wanted to talk to me about Beth for the book she was writing. I thought it might very well come out under our imprint over here. But I don't understand–'

'The only motive the police or any of us can think of for Phoebe's murder is blackmail.'

'Blackmail!'

'Phoebe stole a document from the Senate House Library and it is quite possible she used it to blackmail someone and was killed because of that.'

'But what has this to do with me?'

'If Beth had found out about the East European editions – and she might well have done in the same way that I did, someone might have written to her – then perhaps she wrote a letter to you about it, a letter that, for some reason, she never sent and which got put in with her other papers, the papers that are now in the library.'

'Yes, but–'

'Phoebe was working on those papers. If she'd found something like that, then she might quite possibly have been blackmailing you. Well then, if all this was made public you wouldn't only have been in trouble with the law – forgery and appropriation of funds – but you'd also lose all your other authors. Who would trust you?'

'I see.'

'You must admit that it gives you a motive for murdering Phoebe.'

Ralph moved the paperknife a fraction to the left. 'I suppose it does,' he said.

'So where were you on the twenty-seventh?'

'Is that when she was killed?'

'Yes.'

He opened a drawer of the desk and took out a large desk diary. 'The twenty-seventh?' He flipped over the pages. 'On the twenty-seventh I went to Oxford to see one of my authors, Robert Drummond. You probably know his work.'

'So that's fine. You have an alibi.'

'Unfortunately, no. He wasn't there. I later learned that he had been called away unexpectedly and hadn't been able to get in touch with me.'

'So what did you do?'

'Wandered around the bookshops, had some lunch, then I caught the late afternoon train back to London. Alas, I fear I met no one I knew, so no one can confirm what I say. However, I do most earnestly assure you that I did not kill that unfortunate young woman, nor was she blackmailing me.'

I didn't reply and he said, 'I hope you believe me.'

'Well,' I said, 'I would have thought that if you had killed Phoebe you'd have had a better alibi than that. Unless it's a sort of double bluff.'

He looked at me coldly. 'It certainly is not.'

We sat in silence for a while, neither of us, I felt, knowing quite what to say. Eventually Ralph asked, 'What do you propose to do?'

'Do?'

'About – about the East European rights.'

'Oh, I see. Are you in a position to repay the money now?'

'Yes, I could do that.'

'Then perhaps you should tell John. He – or rather his business – also has a liquidity problem at the moment and I think he'd welcome a substantial cash sum. Being in the same position himself might make him more sympathetic to what you've done. Besides, I don't think he'd want the publicity of a court case.'

'I see. Thank you, Sheila, for your advice. I am very grateful. And you–?

'I'll leave it up to John,' I said. 'It really has nothing to do with me.'

'That is very generous of you.'

I picked up my handbag and prepared to depart. 'As I said before, I won't be writing a Life of Beth – it would hardly be appropriate in the circumstances. Actually, I don't think the family will want anything like that in the near future. I suggest you get in touch with Ruth Taylor at St Hilda's. I think she'd be the most suitable person to do a critical study of Beth's work, if she is willing, that is.'

'I am sure she will do an excellent job.'

'I've finished editing the short stories. I'll do the Introduction when I get back to Taviscombe. I should be able to let you have it by the end of next month.'

'Thank you very much. I will look forward to that.'

'What an extremely distasteful episode!' Hilda said, when I told her what had happened. 'I do feel it is your duty to expose his fraud, for the sake of his other authors.'

'I don't somehow think he'll ever try that sort of thing again.'

'No, perhaps not. Nevertheless, I don't think he should be allowed to get away with it scot-free.'

I laughed. 'I think having to admit it all to me, having to lose face like that, was quite a punishment for him! Anyway, it's up to John, really.'

'And do you think it *was* a sufficient motive for murder?' Hilda asked.

'I don't know,' I said thoughtfully. 'As I said, I'd have thought he'd have a proper alibi if he *had* done it.'

'I don't know. There was no obvious connection between him and Phoebe Walters – no reason for anyone to suspect him.'

'That's true. But actually, if he had killed her, I really can't see him doing it that way. I mean, hiring a van and running someone down – that's not Ralph's style at all!'

'Well, you know him better than I do, but it does seem to me that he's the only person we know of who has a really substantial motive.'

'That's assuming there *was* something about the East European contracts among Beth's papers,' I reminded her. 'We don't actually know that.'

'That is so, but it is still more than we have against anyone else.'

The following day I had a phone call from Nicola.

'Just to let you know that Ben and I are off to the States next week,' she said.

'Lovely! I do hope you enjoy it. I love America – I always feel so *well* when I'm over there! So, have you any more news from the police? They didn't object to you both leaving the country?'

She laughed. 'No, no problem. Actually, from what Sergeant Mortimer said when I spoke to him last, it looks as if they're beginning to wonder if Phoebe *was* murdered.'

'What!'

'Well,' Nicola said, 'they seem to think it might have just been a hit-and-run thing after all.'

'But–'

'They think the Bedford van they found – the one that knocked her down – might have been bought by someone who was going to use it for a robbery or something and then, when the accident happened, they panicked and just ditched it.'

'I see.'

'It would make sense, wouldn't it?'

'Yes, I suppose it would.'

'Actually, I rather hope that's the end of it. Ben's been pretty upset about it all. I know he was very scathing about Phoebe, but she was his sister after all. And he hadn't told his father that it might be murder, he just said there'd been an accident. He was dreading having to go back and tell him. No, really, it would be a relief all round!'

'That's true.'

'Besides, there was never any real motive, was there? I mean, all that stuff about a stolen document – it was a bit far-fetched, wasn't it!'

'Yes, perhaps it was. Well, have a lovely time in America.'

'I'll send you a postcard of the Liberty Bell!'

'A relief all round,' I said to Hilda. 'I suppose it would be.'

'*If*,' she said caustically, 'you could bring yourself to accept such a simple solution.'

'What do you think?' I asked. 'Do you think that's how it was?'

'I don't know. Probably no one ever will know.' She looked at me enquiringly. 'You're not satisfied, though, are you?'

I shook my head. 'No, not really. It *is* a simple solution. Fine, if everything in life was black and white, but there seem to me so many grey areas in all this, so many ifs and buts. I just have this peculiar feeling–'

'What sort of feeling?'

'As though I've got a lot of pieces, and if only I could fit them together, then I'd know exactly what happened. It keeps niggling away.'

'Well,' Hilda said, 'perhaps you should make one final effort to put the pieces together.'

'Perhaps. I can't help thinking that Beth's strange novel is at the root of the matter. I feel that if only I could work out who the hero is meant to be, I'd solve the whole thing.'

Hilda took off her reading glasses and put them in their case. 'Well, then,' she said, 'do the thing you're good at.'

'What do you mean?'

'Literary analysis. Really examine your text. You've always said that one of Beth Blackmore's great strengths as a writer was her ear for dialogue and her ability to catch a tone of voice. Well, then, now's your chance to prove it.'

'You may be right,' I said. 'I'll give it a go.'

I got up and fetched the manuscript and laid it open on the table.

'I'll leave you to it,' Hilda said. 'I've got this new book about Ribbentrop I want to read, so I'll have an early night.' She went over to the sofa and picked up a somnolent Tolly. 'I'll take his lordship with me in case he wakes up and wants to tear the place apart. Good hunting!'

I began to turn the pages of the manuscript, reading it this time not as a novel, but trying to break it down into its component parts of language, listening for echoes of a voice that I knew. For a while it was awkward, difficult, even, but then I stopped trying to do it scientifically and let the words and speech rhythms speak to me. About halfway through the book I suddenly knew that I had solved it. A familiar voice became more and more apparent, so that it seemed that I must have been deaf and stupid not to have heard it before.

I straightened up. My shoulders were stiff from hunching over the manuscript and I had a thumping headache, but I felt an immense surge of satisfaction at having solved the enigma. I looked at the clock. It said one-thirty, but I wasn't in the least bit tired. Now that I had a name, I found I could fit together other pieces of the puzzle. Things that had been lying about in my mind, separate items and incidents, slotted easily into place. On an impulse I got out my diary and studied the underground map. Yes, it all added up. Whether I had got the details right I couldn't tell, but I was quite certain that I now knew who had killed Phoebe Walters and that it definitely was murder.

For a while, the excitement of discovery and satisfaction at my own cleverness outweighed everything else, but then, when I began to contemplate the result I had arrived at, I was appalled. I got up slowly and went into the kitchen to get some water

331

to take an aspirin. What I had was a theory, a theory about which I was absolutely certain, although there was no actual, hard evidence. What I now found difficult to face up to was the fact that, if my theory was correct, several people were going to be devastated and their lives destroyed. I told myself that was not my affair, that the truth must come out, that the guilty must be punished, but I couldn't push away all the implications of my discovery.

I took the aspirin and stood looking at the files and papers on the table. I opened one of the folders and stood for some time looking at the photograph I had retrieved from Phoebe's file, the photograph of us all in the punt at Oxford. I thought of Beth then and of the person she had become, of my own life and how hope blossoms and then dies, also of what remains, and I knew what I had to do.

Chapter Sixteen

I didn't sleep much and was up very early. Even though it was so early, I telephoned Bill North.

'Bill? It's Sheila Malory here.'

'Sheila?' His voice was full of sleep. 'What's the matter, what's happened?'

'I'm so sorry to ring you at this unearthly hour,' I said, 'but as it's Saturday I thought you might be going up to your constituency and I needed to catch you before you went.'

'Yes.' He still sounded bewildered. 'I've got to go up later this morning. Sheila, what is it?'

'Something has happened about Phoebe Walters's murder and I need to see you urgently.'

'What is it?'

'I can't explain over the phone,' I said.

'Can you come here?'

'Where are you?'

I gave him the address.

'Yes, well, I suppose I could call in on my way–'

'Please do, Bill, it's very important.'

He arrived about mid-morning.

'Now what on earth is all this about?' he asked.

'Please sit down, Bill. This may take a little time.'

He sat down on the sofa and I took the chair opposite to him.

'I might as well come straight to the point,' I said. 'I know that you were the person Beth was having an affair with.'

'What? Oh, come on, Sheila.' He laughed. 'This is ridiculous!'

'Alas, no. I'm afraid it's deadly serious. Since it was because Phoebe Walters found out about the affair that she had to be killed.'

The smile left his face and he looked at me coldly.

'I can't imagine what you think you're talking about.'

'Do you want me to explain?'

'Please do, if you think you can.'

'Right. You and Beth were, as I say, having an affair. Somehow a document – a letter to you from Beth, or the other way round – got mixed up in Beth's papers and Phoebe found it. Being the sort of person she was, she saw an excellent opportunity for blackmail. You knew that if you once gave in to her demands there would be others, so you decided to kill her. You arranged to meet her at – I think – Ealing Common station and, straight after answering your ministerial questions in the House, you went to Ealing by tube. You'd previously bought a second-hand Bedford van from a backstreet garage and left it parked on the Common. Am I right so far?'

'Go on.'

'When you'd met Phoebe and got the document in exchange for some money, you followed her in the van and, on that deserted part of the Common, you drove the van full tilt at her and ran her down. Then you drove the van to Hammersmith and left it there, got back on to the tube and returned to Westminster in time for the early evening vote.'

'This is all fantasy.'

'I agree, it does sound fantastic. But what is not fantasy is the fact that when you were searching for some loose change that lunchtime in the National Gallery, you pulled out of the pocket of your leather jacket a set of keys for a Bedford van. You tried very hard to divert my attention away from them to the cigarettes and, at the time, you succeeded. But, later, when I was putting two and two together, I remembered them. I imagine you wore the leather jacket – your disguise, I think you called it – when you went to buy the van, and an old pair of jeans and a baseball cap, and gloves, of course, because of the fingerprints. The man in the garage said the person who bought the van had a North Country accent. I'll always remember your First Grave-Digger in that OUDS production of *Hamlet* – you played him with a Geordie accent; it was brilliant.'

I paused and looked across at him. His face was expressionless.

'One thing struck me. All the places involved were on the District line: Westminster, Acton Town, where you bought the van, Ealing Common, where the murder was committed, and Hammersmith, where you dumped the van.'

'So?'

'It was convenient for you, wasn't it? Especially since you had so little time in every case. I imagine all your movements are pretty well accounted for, your PPS and all the others would be keeping track of where you were, so time was of the essence and the underground – as well as being anonymous – was very convenient.' I paused for a moment. 'But there is one thing you may not have thought of. I expect you automatically used the House of Commons entrance to Westminster underground station and I am quite sure that the policemen on duty on the days in question would remember you coming and going. They're very good at that sort of thing – it's part of their job.'

For the first time, his eyes didn't meet mine and he shifted uneasily and I knew that I had guessed that part correctly and that now he was frightened.

'Well then, am I right?'

He leaned back against the sofa and seemed suddenly to relax, as if some sort of burden had been lifted from him.

'You have absolutely no proof,' he said.

'I know.'

'How did you discover about Beth and me?'

I told him about going through the manuscript and he threw back his head and laughed. 'Good God! Miss Marple meets F.R. Leavis! I always said you were bright. You never had the ability to pursue an argument that Beth had, nor her clear, logical mind, but I remember how you used to make these intuitive leaps that landed you where we both were without going through any of the thought processes. I see you're still at it!'

He sat in silence for a while and then seemed to come to a decision.

'Beth and I met by chance in Athens a couple of years ago. She was visiting Arnold and I was with some commission or other. We had dinner together and, whether it was the ouzo or the moonlight on the Acropolis, we both started reminiscing about Oxford and the time we both fancied we were in love with each other, and – well, one thing led to another. I suppose we were both trying to recapture our lost youth. Whenever either of us could get away we went to Greece, it was only ever in Greece – either to one of the islands or the remoter part of the Mani – places where we wouldn't run into anyone we knew. That day on Hydra, when Helen's friend saw us, was a mistake. I'd forgotten that it was on the tourist route, but that day I realized that we were taking too many risks. When we got back I told Beth that we had to finish it.' He paused and shook his head, as if trying to dispel unpleasant thoughts. 'This is the difficult bit. She was very, very upset. I hadn't realized how seriously she'd taken it all. She wanted us both to get divorced and to marry!'

'You didn't feel like that?'

'Frankly, no. I was fond of Beth, and picking up where we left off all those years ago gave me a bit of a buzz, but nothing more. In any case, I didn't think my father-in-law would like the idea of my dumping his only daughter, and with the power of the press, it wouldn't have done my career any good.'

'Poor Beth.'

'Yes, well. But honestly, I'd never ever pretended that it was anything more than an affair. I *never* promised her anything else. Anyway, she kept on telephoning me and leaving messages to call her. It was getting awkward. Finally I did call her and I'm afraid I was a bit brutal, well, I had to be. I told her it was all over and she had to accept it. She became hysterical – floods of tears and reproaches. Finally I couldn't stand any more and I put the phone down. A few days after that I heard she was dead. The paper the Walters girl found was a letter that Beth wrote to me and which she'd never posted. It was pretty well over the top, saying that she couldn't live without me – that sort of thing – and begging me to see her again. You can imagine how I felt!'

'You think she killed herself?'

'Either that or else she got the tablets mixed up because she was so wound up and emotional. Either way I felt responsible for her death.'

'And Phoebe was blackmailing you.'

'Yes. You can imagine the sort of field day the tabloids would have had: "Love rat North drives mistress to suicide!" My career and my marriage would both be over – my father-in-law would see to that. I was desperate.'

'So you killed her.'

He nodded. 'More or less as you worked it out. I left the House straight after I'd made my statement – fortunately there weren't many questions, so I was away by four o'clock and I was back again by seven for the early evening vote.'

'I see,' I said. 'They don't give any times for things in Hansard – I looked you up for that day – so I didn't realize you'd have been able to get there and back in the time.'

Bill smiled wryly. 'You were very thorough.' He paused for a moment, then he said, 'The awful bit was having to get out after I'd knocked her down and remove the blackmail money from her handbag. Fortunately there was no one about, but it was a tricky moment. I mean, I didn't dare leave it, someone would have asked questions. Apart from that, it all seemed pretty foolproof. I suppose it would have been if it hadn't been for those bloody keys. I was in a rush when I got back, and in a bit of a state, too, as you can imagine, so I didn't think about getting rid of them. Then I simply forgot all about them, and I didn't have any occasion to wear that jacket until the day I met you. The rest you know.'

'Poor Phoebe, too,' I said.

'She was a nasty piece of work and, from what you told me, it doesn't look as though she'll be greatly missed.'

'She was a human being,' I pointed out. 'You killed a human being.'

Bill didn't reply, but sat on the sofa, apparently lost in thought. After a moment he said, 'As I said before, you have no proof, no hard evidence. There's nothing you can do.'

'Not quite nothing,' I said, getting to my feet. 'The press doesn't care much about facts. It thrives on innuendo and rumour. It is also very careful not to go over the edge into anything actually libellous. But rumour and innuendo have brought down more powerful people than you.'

His face was hard. 'Are you blackmailing me, Sheila?'

'I don't want money, if that's what you mean. But you would hardly expect me to condone murder.'

He got up slowly and stood facing me. For a moment I felt very afraid.

Then the door, which had been slightly ajar, was pushed open and Tolly burst into the room and began sharpening his claws ostentatiously on the sofa. I felt the tension drain out of me as I went over and picked him up.

'Who else knows about all this?' Bill asked.

'My cousin Hilda,' I said, 'and I have also written it all down and put it in a safe place.'

Bill smiled. 'You've been reading too much John Buchan,' he said.

We both sat down again. 'I am most desperately sorry about Beth,' Bill said. 'And about poor Helen, too. That was my fault, I suppose. Then there's Anne and the children. It really is the most ghastly mess.' I didn't say anything and he went on. 'Don't worry, Sheila, I'll sort things out. I'll do my best to make it all right. Will you trust me?'

I nodded.

'Very well.' He stood up and held out his hand. 'Goodbye.'

My arms were full of wriggling Siamese cat so I didn't respond to his gesture, but simply said, 'Goodbye Bill.'

When he had gone I sat down on the sofa again with Tolly, suddenly quiet, on my lap. As I mechanically stroked the soft white fur, I wondered if I had done the right thing. Or, if not, what else I could have done.

It was on the late television news that night.

'The death has occurred of Mr Bill North ... accident on the M6 in Staffordshire ... no other vehicle involved ... statement from Downing Street ... this tragic accident ... able Minister ... great loss to the country ... leaves a wife and three children...'

Bill had sorted it out.

'Well, that's it,' I said to Hilda. 'God, what a terrible waste the whole thing is.'

Hilda murmured agreement, but she was

preoccupied. Tolly, who was never allowed out at night, had slipped out and, after three hours, still hadn't come back.

'I only opened the front door a crack to put the milk bottles out,' Hilda was lamenting, 'and he was out like a flash.'

'Let's go and have one more look,' I said. I was glad to have something to do to take my mind off the dreadful thing that had happened.

We looked round the gardens once again, shining a torch into the shrubs and bushes. We wandered up and down the adjacent streets, calling 'Tolly-Wolly-Tolly, Tim-timtim' and rattling the cat-treat tin. But to no avail.

'He'll be all right,' I said for the umpteenth time. 'He's probably just round the corner watching us, laughing his socks off.'

'Yes, I know,' Hilda said forlornly. 'I'm sure you're right. But you do hear such terrible things–'

'You go to bed. He'll be there waiting to

be let in when you come down in the morning. Foss does it all the time.'

I finally persuaded her upstairs and I went to bed myself. I couldn't sleep, though. I tossed and turned and tried not to think of the day's events, but it all went round and round in my mind, memories of Beth as a young girl, happy, frivolous days at Oxford, Bill speaking at the Union, acting at the Playhouse, days on the river – and then Bill's face when he told me about Phoebe, the hardness of his voice, the lack of concern about what he had done. How had he changed so much? He had become cold and ruthless, caring only for his career and the power that it had brought him. He killed Phoebe to protect all that and he had killed himself to preserve his reputation when his career was in ruins. He had married Anne for the sake of her father's influence and he had abandoned Beth when she seemed to threaten his political future. And poor Beth, too, snatching at happiness without thought for anyone else. Did we all become selfish and hardened as we left youth behind and clung on to what remained of our lives?

I gradually drifted into an uneasy sleep, only to be woken by a noise downstairs. I looked at the clock and saw that it was two-thirty. Reluctantly I got up and put on my dressing gown. The light was on in the kitchen. Hilda was sitting at the kitchen table watching a totally unrepentant Tolly demolishing a plate of fish. She looked up as I opened the door. Her face was radiant.

'Oh Sheila, did we disturb you? I couldn't sleep so I came down just one more time and there he was, bless him, waiting patiently to be let in!'

Tolly raised his face momentarily from his dish and gave me what can only be described as a smirk.

'I'm *so* glad!'

The dish was now licked clean and Hilda picked Tolly up in her arms and laid her face against the soft white fur.

'Wicked boy!' she said. 'Giving us all such a fright.'

She raised her head and I saw that there were tears in her eyes. Who was it said that love was the devil and all? It had killed Beth and Bill North, and Phoebe Walters, of course. It had nearly killed poor Helen. *Amor omnia vincit.*

'All's well that ends well,' I said with a briskness that I was far from feeling. 'What do you say to a nice cup of tea?'

The publishers hope that this book has given you enjoyable reading. Large Print Books are especially designed to be as easy to see and hold as possible. If you wish a complete list of our books please ask at your local library or write directly to:

Magna Large Print Books
Magna House, Long Preston,
Skipton, North Yorkshire.
BD23 4ND

This Large Print Book for the partially sighted, who cannot read normal print, is published under the auspices of
THE ULVERSCROFT FOUNDATION

THE ULVERSCROFT FOUNDATION

... we hope that you have enjoyed this Large Print Book. Please think for a moment about those people who have worse eyesight problems than you ... and are unable to even read or enjoy Large Print, without great difficulty.

You can help them by sending a donation, large or small to:

The Ulverscroft Foundation, 1, The Green, Bradgate Road, Anstey, Leicestershire, LE7 7FU, England.
or request a copy of our brochure for more details.

The Foundation will use all your help to assist those people who are handicapped by various sight problems and need special attention.

Thank you very much for your help.